The Executioner reached the rail and vaulted over

He bent his knees to cushion the fall, then tucked and rolled.

At the far stairs, gunmen were struggling to separate themselves from each other. One of them spotted the Executioner and pulled a pistol, but Bolan locked his gun's sight on his opponent and triggered a short, precision burst.

Even as his bullets whizzed past Bolan's ear, the gunman became nothing more than useless weight snarling up the other men.

Bolan charged the group and quickly disarmed one of them, turning the weapon around and ramming the stock into its former owner's head. Next Bolan clubbed a third gunman into unconsciousness before another man climbing the stairs reached out and jabbed his thumb into the warrior's eye with a lucky grope.

The Executioner staggered, clutching his burning eye. He willed himself back into the fight and grabbed his attacker's wrist. With all of his strength and leverage, Bolan twisted and hauled the man to the ground, bouncing him face-first off the concrete.

Up the stairs, Bolan found the wisest of the bunch lying still, fighting to keep his entrails inside his belly. The warrior reached into his first-aid kit, pulled out the gauze he had and pressed it against the bullet wound. The wounded gunman's eyes were wide with confusion, but Bolan kept direct pressure on the wound.

"You'll survive," Bolan told him. "Just make sure that Kilo and Tonne know there's something more lethal than them in West Palm Beach tonight."

MACK BOLAN ®
The Executioner

The Executioner
Don Pendleton's ®

DOUBLE CROSS

A GOLD EAGLE BOOK FROM

WORLDWIDE ®

TORONTO • NEW YORK • LONDON
AMSTERDAM • PARIS • SYDNEY • HAMBURG
STOCKHOLM • ATHENS • TOKYO • MILAN
MADRID • WARSAW • BUDAPEST • AUCKLAND

Recycling programs
for this product may
not exist in your area.

First edition April 2013

ISBN-13: 978-0-373-64413-1

Special thanks and acknowledgment to
Douglas Wojtowicz for his contribution to this work.

DOUBLE CROSS

Printed in U.S.A.

Power is no blessing in itself, except when it is used to protect the innocent.

—Jonathan Swift
1667–1745

I have a calling to not only punish the guilty, but to protect the innocent. And I will move heaven and earth to do so.

—Mack Bolan

THE
MACK BOLAN
LEGEND

Nothing less than a war could have fashioned the destiny of the man called Mack Bolan. Bolan earned the Executioner title in the jungle hell of Vietnam.

But this soldier also wore another name—Sergeant Mercy. He was so tagged because of the compassion he showed to wounded comrades-in-arms and Vietnamese civilians.

Mack Bolan's second tour of duty ended prematurely when he was given emergency leave to return home and bury his family, victims of the Mob. Then he declared a one-man war against the Mafia.

He confronted the Families head-on from coast to coast, and soon a hope of victory began to appear. But Bolan had broken society's every rule. That same society started gunning for this elusive warrior—to no avail.

So Bolan was offered amnesty to work within the system against terrorism. This time, as an employee of Uncle Sam, Bolan became Colonel John Phoenix. With a command center at Stony Man Farm in Virginia, he and his new allies—Able Team and Phoenix Force—waged relentless war on a new adversary: the KGB.

But when his one true love, April Rose, died at the hands of the Soviet terror machine, Bolan severed all ties with Establishment authority.

Now, after a lengthy lone-wolf struggle and much soul-searching, the Executioner has agreed to enter an "arm's-length" alliance with his government once more, reserving the right to pursue personal missions in his Everlasting War.

1

"We are live at the conclusion of one of the most explosive trials in Florida's history," Zoe Sifuentes said, holding the microphone close to her face. Outside the courthouse, the wind flicked her silken black hair carelessly. She turned, looking toward the convoy of black-and-white SUVs with the bade of the West Palm Beach police department emblazoned on the white doors.

Zoe brushed her hair from where it was pressed to her chin by the breeze, big brown eyes scanning the arrival. There was a gray-white school bus, its windows reinforced with a grim black latticework of steel bars, tucked between the third and fourth vehicles of the WPBPD convoy. Motorcycle officers, six of them, were astride their big Harley Davidson motorcycles.

The police were out in full force, and if they weren't enough, then there were black SUVs shadowing the convoy that came to a halt, and the men who exited them wore black, crisp suits and dark glasses that made their sockets look bottomless. These had to either be the FBI or the United States Marshal's service. Either way, she could make out the presence of powerful automatic weapons in their possession.

Once again Zoe was reminded how much of a menace the Chief Dozen—the most merciless faction of Le Loupe Grotte—had been to West Palm Beach, Florida. Le Loupe Grotte was a statewide cancer that had been operating uncontested since the mid-'90s, but the Chief Dozen were a group of the worst of the worst—the hardest cored members of the Haitian gang sent to take control of the city of West Palm Beach.

Fifty homicides in 2007, including a full-on blazing gun battle at a crowded shopping mall on Christmas Eve, had been tied to the gang. For the Chief Dozen, the response from law enforcement was as total and dominating as humanly possible. The only failure that the police and Feds had encountered was that two of the "dozen" who were at the top of the Haitian mob army were missing, presumed dead. The two men had been chased into one of their warehouses, a volatile drug lab that had exploded violently. Charred skeletal remains, left so brittle by the intense heat of the ensuing blaze, crumbled even as they were gently picked up to be put into evidence bags.

Zoe didn't feel sorry for those two men.

She knew their names. Emile Kilo and Ian Tonne, a deadly pair who had been nicknamed Kiloton on the street, not just for the compression of their names, but for the fact that they were as deadly as a small nuclear warhead. It had been the two of them who had led the fight at the mall.

While Zoe hadn't been on the scene for that, she'd managed to grab a cameraman and head to that final, fatal standoff against Kiloton. She'd arrived just in time to see a fireball blossom from the side of the warehouse, and stayed to watch it burn to the ground, rocked by several more shattering detonations of volatile chemicals within.

That had been the beginning of the end for the Chief Dozen, and hopefully with their downfall on the beach, then would come the collapse of Le Loupe Grotte.

"Zoe, quit daydreaming." Rivera, her cameraman, spoke up. She whirled back to face the lens.

"As you can see, the surviving leaders of the Chief Dozen are under heavy guard. The police and federal law enforcement are sparing nothing to make certain that these men will remain locked up for the rest of their lives," Zoe announced on the fly. "Never has Florida been so terrorized by such a small group of men—"

Something made a grunting sound behind her. Zoe wondered at the strange new sound and turned to see a growing puff of dust and debris rising from underneath the prison bus. The police and Feds were on edge, aiming their weapons at the ground from where the jet of detritus came from. Some were on the radio when a second grunt resounded.

This time Zoe was looking right at the source of the sound. It was a weird flex of the asphalt, formed by a ring, as if some pressure were acting on the stone so as to make it ripple like the surface of a calm pond. She wondered what kind of force could do that when the ring suddenly slurped down under the ground, vomiting up a thick column of dust.

The column of dust was accompanied by a fierce wind that pushed her, almost toppling her off her high-heeled shoes. Luckily, she was in slacks. If she'd been in a tight skirt, she never would have had the freedom of movement to recover her balance. Just as suddenly as the wind struck, she was blind, enveloped in the cloud disgorged by the new hole in the street.

She gave a shout, but as the wave of crackles filled the air, Zoe knew that her voice would be lost in the chatter of gunfire as she was lost behind the billows of dust and debris. Knowing better than to stand in proximity of a gunfight, she threw herself flat, dropping the microphone and covering her head with both hands. She could feel sprays of pebbles and splinters of asphalt striking the backs of her hands. A line of slugs must have ripped along close to her.

This was some serious shit going on. It sounded like she was back embedded with Marines in Fallujah, except she wasn't protected by a bulletproof vest or heavy Kevlar helmet. That wouldn't matter, though, not if the Palm Beach cops, armed with their HK's—she suddenly remembered that they were called G-36s—could direct violent and swift counterfire.

The rattle of weapons faded for a moment, the dust beginning to clear. That's when she saw a sudden column of white, swirling gasses punch through the dust cloud, punctuated by a teeth-shaking explosion that made her bury her head once more, hot fragments of metal and fiberglass raining all around her. She could smell the stench of burning hair, and the accompanying sudden stab of pain informed her that it was her own hair burning.

Zoe rolled onto her back, smothering the beginnings of the flames, more debris popping against her face and chest. She kept her eyes shut, one forearm across her face to protect her. It was as if someone had crushed a van between his enormous hands, breaking it down to powder and flakes like they were salt crackers, then let the leftover bits drain between his fingers.

Another ground-rumbling explosion ripped through the air. A third followed immediately.

The gunfire rose once more, an incessant head-pounding cacophony that rocked her brutally. Here and there, in brief lulls between eruptions and gunfire, she could hear screams and panic.

Zoe cast around, reaching for her cameraman. If they stayed out in the open, they were doomed to catch something in the crossfire.

She touched wet, sticky hair. She explored further, one finger sinking into a gaping crater among the strands, and Zoe had to fight off the urge to vomit. She'd poked what was left over when a bullet had destroyed a human brain. She jerked violently away from the cored human skull, and in an instant saw that it was Rivera. His camera was shattered, blasted to pieces.

Either the gunman who had shot him thought the TV camera was a weapon, or it was just a reckless act among the mad slaughter in the streets. Either way, Zoe scurried toward the cover of a concrete planter. Bullets buzzed over her head, and through the clearing smoke and dust, she noticed a group of dark men carrying all manner of heavy weaponry. She bit her lower lip at the sight of them, knowing that this had to be Le Loupe Grotte trying to free their friends in a full-blown military-like operation.

She heard shouts in French, confirming her theory. The brutal battle raged on the street, bullets shredding cars and bodies alike. Gouts of flame and boiling smoke rose from the explosive hammered shells of the FBI or Marshal SUVs, again reminding her of the wreckage she'd seen in the midst of an Iraq war firefight. The only thing that could smash and implode a vehicle like that, turning a Chevy Suburban into what looked like a burning two-seater convertible coupe, was a rocket-propelled grenade, the RPG-7 that the Iraqis had inherited from their Soviet suppliers or had smuggled across Syrian and Iranian borders by foreign nationals.

The grenade launchers turned this assault into a one-sided battle, as far as she could see. Cops and feds wouldn't have the freedom of loosing an armor-piercing warhead on a city street. They were stuck with merely automatic rifles and submachine guns.

"Only machine guns," she said aloud as she ducked her head. Zoe couldn't believe that full-auto was the *weak* end of a gun battle.

Something struck the other side of the concrete tree planter she was crouched behind and suddenly Zoe was flying, limbs flailing through empty air, the world twirling in her vision. As she spun, hurled from her hiding spot, she saw the expanding cloud that marked the impact of another rocket-propelled grenade. Despite being shielded by a ton of concrete and solid dirt, the concussive force of the detonation threw her like a rag doll.

Zoe didn't have to tell herself to go loose. The blast wave left her numb, and as she slammed into the sidewalk, her limbs were rubbery. Even as her head bounced on the ground, she didn't feel anything. Maybe she was numb from the sheer overpressure produced by the RPG warhead, or maybe her spinal cord had been severed, leaving the rest of her body as a separate entity, a phantom chained by meat to her intellect.

Sensation returned to her like a sheet of hurricane-force rain, falling upon her and making her wish that she *had* been paralyzed.

As far as Zoe could tell, however, she could still move, arms and legs responding to her mental commands, but she was in no hurry to get up. Instead, she willed herself to remain flattened. Her journalistic instincts gave protest to missing what could be the most important law-enforcement event in Florida history, but the truth was that she wanted to live.

Even at the worst of her time with the Marine expeditionary force in Iraq, she had never been subjected to the mayhem that this Haitian attack produced. Her eyes looked upward, and she realized that she'd been thrown clear of the cloud of smoke and dust. She was drawn into the clear blue skies of West Palm Beach, decorated here and there with faint wispy contrails of airplanes flying overhead, miles above this battle-racked spot of ground.

Out of the corner of her eye she noticed a pair of legs, feet clad in combat boots, grow closer. Zoe stared, not reacting to the approaching person. Either it was an EMT or a cop, in which case her injuries would be tended to, or it was one of the Haitian wolf men, cleaning up witnesses.

A face bent over her line of sight, deep brown features obscuring the blue sky. Knotted shoelaces of braided hair hung around the man's face. A beard that at first seemed neatly trimmed, but was actually itself braided into two long, writhing tentacles of knot-tamed hair, dangled from his chin. Eyes as black as night blinked momentarily beneath a pair of bushy eyebrows.

"You can quit faking, pretty lady," the patois-tinged words fell from his full lips. "I was hoping you'd still be alive."

Zoe couldn't speak. Her throat was paralyzed, but this time she knew the cause. She was racked with terror, stunned into silence by the familiarity of the man bent over her.

It was Emile Kilo, one of the men that Florida authorities had assumed dead. Zoe herself tried to analyze how she had been present at his funeral pyre, wondering how he could have survived such a lethal inferno.

Kilo reached down, rough, calloused fingers brushing her cheek. He turned her head left, then right, watching her wince. "Good. Your neck's not broken. You'll still be useful."

With that, he rested a small, hand-held digital video camera on her chest, letting it rest in the notch between her bra-constrained breasts.

"You take this to your boss. You show this video. We run this world now," Kilo said softly.

For a man so violent, so scraggly looking, his voice was gentle, as was his touch. He looked as if he'd been dragged down miles of rough road, scars crisscrossing his mahogany flesh, old wounds forming a yellowish-orange spiderweb that described a history of brutality to himself and others. That was what stuck out of the body armor and crisp, black battle-dress uniform.

He stood straight, and Zoe followed him with her eyes. It was as if the head and mane of some humanoid lion were resting on the shoulders of a futuristic soldier. Kilo unfolded a pair of sunglasses and put them on as he looked up to the sky.

"The spirits are with us, *Madame* Sifuentes," Kilo said absently. "No mortal can stand between us and freedom."

Zoe coughed, gathering up the strength to speak.

"Don't talk." Kilo cut her off, looking down at her. His sunglasses dropped a little and she could see his black irises against the white sclera of his orbs, like some kind of sick, negative sunset as they were bisected by the black frames and lenses of the glasses. "You are listening to the testimony of Kiloton and the Chief Dozen. Your input, your questions, are irrelevant."

Cold fear poured through Zoe's veins.

"Play the DVD. Be enlightened. And make your choice," Kilo told her.

With that, he turned and walked away.

Zoe finally sat up after what felt like an eternity. Behind her, in front of the courthouse, it was a scene of widespread destruction. Bodies and crushed vehicles were scattered around, the broken toys of an insane giant. Even the courthouse itself bled smoke and fire through brutal wounds torn through its facade.

The camera rolled down into her hands and she looked at it, a normally inoffensive little silver-skinned box with a black lens on one end, a folded view screen tucked down to make it slim, pocket-size.

It really only weighed ounces, but it felt massive. She couldn't lift it, as if it had its own poisonous, dark atmosphere of evil, the air of some demonic realm where Kilo had risen from the dead and stayed while the world of man assumed he'd burned and died. Inside this innocent little block of silver-colored plastic was the testimony of a walking devil, the living dead arisen and killing on the streets of West Palm Beach.

Zoe Sifuentes prayed that there was something, someone who could ward off such a monster.

Hundreds of miles away, in a cavern on the Southern California coast named Strong Base One, a soldier between missions stirred, as much as from the news reports escaping Florida as from the cosmic thread of a War Everlasting being plucked.

A prayer was about to be answered, in the form of one Mack Samuel Bolan.

The Executioner was coming to Florida.

HAL BROGNOLA WATCHED the monitor grimly as footage from West Palm Beach played on the monitors. The footage was only an hour old, but the Stony Man Farm staff were close on hand, examining every frame for intelligence data to analyze. So far, the attackers were well coordinated and hid their faces and identities behind gas masks and beneath helmets. They further obscured themselves thanks to clouds of smoke and debris, or by keeping to cover behind mounds of wreckage.

The President, upon seeing such a violent assault on the protectors of law and order, was hot on the phone to Stony Man Farm.

"Hal, I don't want Florida to turn into the next Mexico. We can't allow drug gangs to declare open war on the government," the Man told him over the hotline. "But at the same time, we have to watch out to make certain this doesn't turn into something like Chechnya. If we send troops down…"

"That's why you want Stony Man to engage in an operation," Brognola returned. "This way, we can hunt and kill whoever is responsible without seeming like we're destroying the Constitution."

"Lord knows that I get enough of that unmitigated bullshit poured on me every time I twitch my finger," the President grumbled. "But look at that mess…all those people dead. Good men, doing their jobs…how many orphans were made today?"

"You don't want to know," Brognola told him. "It will eat you up inside."

"Hal, we need to bring down the hammer and bring it down hard," the President said.

Brognola frowned. "Phoenix Force is working in Eastern Europe, and Able Team is up in Alaska, about as far from Florida as humanly possible. We could try to pull Lyons's team in. After all, they're predominantly assigned to operate within the U.S. borders…"

"Hal." Barbara Price spoke up. "You won't have to call either team."

Brognola looked toward her.

"Sorry to interrupt, Mr. President," Price continued.

"Not at all, Ms. Price. Are you insinuating what I believe you are?" the President asked.

"I just received word that Jack Grimaldi is flying in from California," Price stated. "He's not coming to Virginia, but has been asked to go directly to Orlando International Airport."

"How could he be on the case so fast?" the President inquired. "We didn't say a thing yet here at the White House."

"Striker doesn't work in mysterious ways," Brognola replied. "Stony Man Farm is only one set of ears to the ground for him. He's been around the planet a dozen times, picking up all manner of information and contacts."

"What's in Southern California?" the Man asked. "I didn't hear anything about recent…activity there."

Brognola looked to Price. "He has an undisclosed location there. A home away from the Farm. Even we don't know where it is, but we have hot links to it, should we need to find him, and he can call on us at any time."

"You can't find him?" the President asked.

"Which means he can't be found by his enemies—what few survive," Price added. "Obviously, there are those, particularly on the field teams, who may know more, or may not."

"In other words, he's not sharing that information," the President mused. "The man's earned his privacy, and after fighting for America's sake, if not the world's, he's proved that he's simply not going to snap and go on a rampage."

"Oh, if he's on his way to Florida, you can expect a rampage," Brognola stated. "He just isn't going to allow more lawmen or any civilians to come to harm."

"Thank God," the President said. "Keep me up-to-date. Especially if you need interference between the FBI and his efforts."

"As soon as Striker took this case, you, and we, are hands off. He hasn't asked for a cover identity from the Farm, just a quick ride from Jack," Price stated. "Maybe G-Force will stick around, maybe he'll return to base here. Either way, he's gone lone wolf, and is already working on his approach. One not requiring anything more than his wits and on-hand resources."

The President took an audible, deep breath over the phone line. "So we can have rumors of some intergang warfare?"

"Or a lone terrorist going after Le Loupe Grotte," Brognola mused. "Though, Striker could likely dust off his old Mafia Black Ace cover…"

"The mob hasn't been that active in Florida for decades, not with the influx of other immigrant gangs," the President mentioned. "But, given his tactics, he could be pushing for a hard core return to glory."

"The less you think about it, the better," Price told the President. "Just know that he's going to put an end to this or die trying."

There was a long, uncomfortable silence in the Stony Man Farm War Room at the mention of Bolan's possible failure. After all, the Executioner was a human being, one who could be hurt, who could die as easily from a bullet as any other man.

"All luck to him," the President whispered, almost as a prayer.

With that, the Farm's direct line to the Oval Office closed.

"I'm going to have to see what I can do. I'm heading to Florida myself," Brognola told Price. "The FBI and Justice Department are going to need all the help they can get to coordinate the manhunt for the Chief Dozen and the Loupes."

"And you'll be closer to the ground to talk with Striker in the meantime," Price returned.

"You read my mind," Brognola answered. "Just like in the old days, when he was on the run."

"How much interference are you going to run for him?" Price asked.

"Nothing that will keep the FBI and local PD from believing that they're actually avenging their lost friends," Brognola returned.

"Think he'll be expecting you?" Price asked. "Just in case?"

"You know how he works, Barb," Brognola countered. "He's never going to put himself into a situation where he has to bring physical harm close to a lawman or a civilian. And if he does get there, he's done all the somersaults necessary to keep innocents and allies out of the line of fire."

"Give him my love when you see him," Price said.

Brognola nodded. He had a flight to catch. Price turned to make certain his tickets would be waiting for him at Dulles.

2

Mack Bolan had chosen Jack Grimaldi as his pilot for several reasons, most of them having to do with the war bag he was currently checking as he sat in the back of the Gulfstream jet.

As a charter pilot, Grimaldi didn't have to actually land at an airport where there was a terminal. Without having to go through a terminal, Bolan didn't have to go through the effort of clearing his full-auto firearms through customs or airport X-ray machines as he was not on a commercial flight.

The same advantage went toward his usual concealed carry kit of a Beretta 9 mm autoloader and his powerful .44 Magnum Desert Eagle hand cannon. Certainly, Bolan had plenty of identification that would label him as a law-enforcement official, and thus allowed him to carry a firearm aboard a commercial airliner—with certain badges. But the thought of being seated with all of that hardware in a plane seat, in close proximity and rubbing elbows with other passengers, meant that people would become far too curious and cause either trouble in that they believed he was a terrorist himself, or would spread word of a heavily armed Fed arriving on the scene in Florida. That kind of breach of secrecy could compromise his position, and catch others in the crossfire.

Also, given current commercial airline regulations, a last-minute ticket from one side of the country to the other would prove to be a flag-raiser on a commercial carrier. On a chartered flight, all Grimaldi had to do was to file a flight plan and stick with it, and there would be little scrutiny in regard to the journey.

Yet another advantage was that Bolan could communicate freely while in the back of the Gulfstream. On a commercial flight if he tried to phone ahead to gather information or to make hookups, then he would be overheard, and there would also be limits to how freely he could speak in front of others, even in the relative solitude of first class. Currently, Bolan was using his satellite phone to burn up the hotlines to make accommodations with friends and allies, as well as to gather advance information.

This was how the warrior worked, how he was able to act so swiftly after effecting a triage on world crises. So far, an hour and a half into the flight, and just two hours after receiving the first footage from the chaos in West Palm Beach, he'd already set up a safehouse and an automobile for himself.

In between calls, he was at work, studying maps of the area he was entering, including looking at the rest of Palm Beach county. This was refreshing research, bringing facts that he had stored back to the forefront. West Palm, as it was affectionately known, was a metropolitan spread where five and a half million souls lived and worked. It might have seemed a "small" town, the official census barely breaking 100,000, but there was a huge sprawling area, perfect for a criminal organization to move in. That size of a populace was ripe to have a hundred thousand fall through the cracks, living in the shadows of lawful civilization, either dragged down by drug addiction or having thrown themselves into the shadows out of pure malice and antipathy for their fellow humans.

The Chief Dozen, newly freed, had been sent to build an outlying empire there for Le Loupe Grotte, which had grown strong thanks to the influx of Haitian refugees and their death grip on the heroin market in Florida, even before the tragic earthquake that killed thousands and left millions homeless.

Bolan made use of a series of back doors into computer databases made for him by Aaron "the Bear" Kurtzman and other computer-savvy allies to look into the official records on the

Chief Dozen. Luckily, thanks to the now-derailed trial, the district attorney's office had an extensive amount of documentation that was as complete as humanly possible. The prosecution was so thorough simply for the fact that they needed the case against the captured Chief Dozen to be watertight.

It was going to be a powerful read-through, but Bolan downloaded the PDF report detailing the information within. As the PDF format was highly interactive, the Executioner would be able to access and search for specific items with only a few keystrokes. He kept one copy on his heavy-duty laptop, a hand-built machine designed and assembled by Hermann "Gadgets" Schwarz, the technical genius behind Stony Man, and one of Bolan's closest friends and fellow Penetration Team Able veteran. The heavy-duty laptop had a solid-state hard drive, with no magnetic disc within, allowing for massive amounts of data to be stored and accessed with a speed that made traditional hard drives seem as if they were sitting still. The laptop also had a communications suite that allowed internet access and telephone communication from even the most remote areas on the planet.

The real reason, however, the laptop was considered "heavy duty" was that it was constructed within a Kevlar-and-carbon-fiber shell. This particular model had minor smears on its lid from where Bolan had fired an AK-47 at it, the steel-cored 7.62 mm ComBloc rounds stopped and blunted. The electronics, cushioned or overbuilt to withstand even the shock of a full magazine of thirty rounds slamming into it, worked immediately afterward.

Ever since the Executioner had begun his war against the criminals who destroyed his family, he had been working on the bleeding edge of technology, operating alongside veterans of the Jet Propulsion Laboratory on his first War Wagon, utilizing rewritable DVD drives for his data storage while the majority of the world was still slogging along with magnetic media. To stay ahead of those who sought to usurp the rule of law, to further the savagery of Animal Man, Bolan not only required the latest in weaponry, but the latest in communications and information technology.

Forearmed and forewarned, Bolan would not be behind the eight-ball when he went face-to-face with his foes. Research would direct his eyes to the nooks and crannies that would have otherwise been unknown, allow him back doors to escape through that he would have missed and thus been forced to stand and fight, endangering the lives of innocents.

This kind of mental and physical preparation was paramount to Bolan's success over the years. While others would be endlessly bored by looking at words and numbers on a screen, or scrawled into a notebook—what he had done before he'd gathered enough money to have someone build a computer system for him—this was not only vital, but something that kept his attention rapt. It made the hours in the air and the miles traveled fly along even faster.

Bolan's mind was aflame as he absorbed information. He had always been a voracious reader, having devoured Cervantes' *Don Quixote* in his early teens, then rereading it at every opportunity. It was this same insatiable desire for knowledge that had allowed him to learn Italian and Russian to such a level of fluency that he could be mistaken for a native speaker, as well as to gather the basics of other languages to make travels around the globe just a little easier.

A dumb man wouldn't have gone as long as he had, even simply in special operations back in his Army days. He wasn't a genius, but he had a great memory and the willingness to study and arm up on data as well as guns and ammo.

Bolan took a break to relax his eyes before turning to his war bag. Inside he had a few items he had been wringing out at Strong Base One that he felt would be good for working in an urban environment like West Palm's metropolitan area.

Bolan had gathered two weapons chambered in .300 Blackout, both based on the traditional AR-15/M-16 pattern that he'd used faithfully for the length of his military and lone wolf careers. The Blackout cartridge was an update of the .300 Whisper round, a custom hunting bullet designed by J. D. Jones to provide both mass and power for subsonic rounds as well as duplicating and improving upon the ballistics of an AK-47 in an assault rifle platform. A simple change of magazine switch allowed for quiet, close, devastating autofire or long-range precision marksmanship in a rifle with a full-length barrel, while losing very little in terms of punch from an abbreviated pistol or carbine-length pipe.

Indeed, one of the two weapons was an AR-PDW, only a few inches of the gas system pipe covered by a collapsing short stock and a nine-inch barrel. The weapon was named the Honey Badger, and was cutting edge for a compact, concealable submachine gun capable of engaging targets out to 200 yards. The Honey Badger was still in the developmental stages, but Bolan knew the men in charge of the company producing them and had received a "shadow prototype." Though the Executioner had chosen his .44 Magnum Desert Eagle, and its predecessor, the .44 Auto Mag, for the ability to put the power of a rifle in a concealable, one-handed package, the Honey Badger was not only nose-to-nose the equal in terms of velocity and punch to the hand cannons, but actually had a longer range and flatter shooting trajectory. Only the sheer mass of an AR receiver dwarfing even the mighty Desert Eagle would keep it out of a hip holster for Bolan.

However, hanging on a sling under a long jacket would give him a weapon as compact as an Uzi submachine gun but with far more horsepower. The Honey Badger was select-fire, for either precision shooting or building-clearing 800 rounds per minute. And, unlike the normal 5.56 mm caliber AR machine pistols he'd used, the .300 Blackout's efficient use of powder and brass meant that he wouldn't subject himself to muzzle flash burns or blindness when he cut loose with one shot or a full salvo.

The rifle was a collapsing-stock carbine with a hybrid red-dot sight and medium-range precision scope, a combination that allowed fast, close-quarters aiming as well as the ability to take out targets at five hundred yards. This was a 16-inch carbine barrel, and on the end of it was a low-impulse suppressor that allowed for far more stealth than a normal M-16 without the drain on killing power.

The mounted sights were firmly attached to the rifle, and a smaller red-dot scope on the Honey Badger was similarly secure, having proven its stability in extended strings of full-auto fire.

"Sarge, are you sure you don't want me flying backup for you?" Grimaldi asked.

"Sorry, Jack," Bolan returned, loading the rifles into his bag. "Right now, my strategy doesn't include you, and you might be needed for Stony Man operations, like Able's work in Alaska."

He could feel his friend's disappointment. Grimaldi's loyalty extended back to almost the very beginning of the Executioner's War Everlasting, when the Army veteran pilot had been stuck serving as a helicopter chauffeur for criminal gangs. Bolan had given Grimaldi the means to get out of that life, a chance to do something worthwhile, not spreading the disease of drug dealing and racketeering indirectly by taking org-crime bigwigs around the country. Because of that redemption, there was nothing that Grimaldi wouldn't do for him, from crawling in hostile sands on an unsanctioned mission into Iran to dropping a ton of laser-guided ordnance on top of a convoy of scumbags from the relative safety of a ground attack fighter.

Even though he wasn't in the cockpit, Bolan could feel the grim, sullen disappointment radiating off his friend. This was bad. On top of being allies, they were dear, close friends. He hated sidelining Grimaldi, but this plan of attack against a wild, out-of-control Haitian drug gang in central Florida was already spotty enough, planned on the fly without much verification of what was to come.

He did know that the situation in West Palm was going to be a free-for-all. Le Loupe Grotte was sending a message to the authorities aligned against them, and also letting rival drug gangs realize that there was no place for them. Bolan needed his

best agility in the line of fire, and keeping Grimaldi close, even
only leaving him on call at a local airport to provide air support, would expose him to an already crowded airspace laden
with bullets and mayhem.

No, this time the Executioner had to strike alone.

HAL BROGNOLA CHEWED on the butt of his cigar as he watched
the video given to Zoe Sifuentes. She was one of those report-
ers with a strong sense of ethics. The inflammatory statements
made on the disk were a proclamation of doom and gloom that
were laden with curses.

The sickening pair known as Kiloton were on his laptop
screen, standing beside a bound lady cop strapped to a chair.
Both men had knives, and Brognola did his best to tune out
what they were doing to the defenseless woman.

This was their testimony. They proclaimed that they had risen
from the dead, all the while…feeding upon the police woman's
freshly carved, still living flesh.

They displayed rites that were similar to vodun, but as always with criminal gangs, there was a perverse, twisted vari-
ance, a complete denial of ethics and goodness in place for
bokor. Brognola had dealt with such "witch doctors"—both self-
imagined and those who were real—through the wide-spanning
adventures of the Stony Man teams and the Executioner. He
knew what was true of the base religion, and what was a violent
perversion to allow the "worshipers" to justify whatever madness and insanity they desired. The same applied to so-called
Christian and Muslim extremists.

The sight of the law woman's slow torture was nauseating.
He couldn't blot it out, not with the sound of their jaws pulping
bits of skin, fat and muscle they'd pared off her mixed in with
the hateful screed they professed.

Finally, Brognola killed the player and turned to the tran-
script of the video.

The two cannibals had stated their case for their return, their holy writ of taking over the underworld, and that no police officer could dream of stopping them.

Brognola couldn't dismiss the terrible images he'd seen, the lurid, ugly closeups of her sliced uniform, her mutilated chest, her face missing strips of skin and muscle. He could still see a tatter of her uniform blouse with the dangling badge and ID. "Montoya."

He opened his laptop and sent off a query to the Farm. He wanted to know who the officer had been. She was only the first of Kiloton's rampage, and too many more had followed her. Yet, for all the explosive brutality of the rocket and grenade attack, "Montoya's" demise was worse. It was slow, agonizing. Nauseating, simply because she, with her remaining, lidless eye, was watching these two maniacs slurp her flesh through their lips like noodles.

The query was answered.

Elizabeta Montoya, patrol woman for the Miami police department. She was the mother of two, divorced, and had been missing for two weeks.

A cleaned, bleached skeleton had been delivered to police headquarters, along with pieces of uniform and identification. Dental records matched the tentative ID.

She'd been buried that day, a closed-casket funeral.

Her young children hadn't had the chance to see their mother one last time.

An instant message popped up on Brognola's machine. The sender was LaMancha38.

It was a reference to Mack Bolan's laptop, Quixotic one-man crusade against organized crime, the dozens of missions that had shown him not only to be a force of nature but an asset to the forces of law and order that were indispensable. If it hadn't been for Bolan, who took the cover name "LaMancha"—one of the many names for Don Quixote—the Sensitive Operations Group based at Stony Man Farm would have never been assembled.

Brognola instantly recognized his friend's internet identification.

Have you seen the video? was Bolan's question.

Couldn't finish watching it, Brognola replied. Too grisly.

There was a long moment of silence. The head Fed knew that it was likely his friend was multitasking at the moment. Bolan was not someone who moved into an area of operations without study, preparation and familiarization of the battleground.

Who was she? Bolan asked.

Brognola took a deep breath, then forwarded the file on Montoya to him.

I'll get money to her family, Bolan responded.

Brognola was fully aware that as much as Bolan spent on keeping himself supplied in the field, he spent far more on assisting the victims of violence by gathering whatever enemy resources he encountered during his missions and funneling it to accounts that would assist them. It had been a long-standing tradition of the Executioner, who not only came in with cleansing flame to annihilate murderers, but to aid those affected by those cold-blooded killers.

You probably figured I'd be on the task force, Brognola typed.

It's your job. If I have information, you'll get it, Bolan answered.

And what can I give to you? Brognola asked. After all, it doesn't look like you're going to be running this as a Stony Man operation.

This is justice for the murdered and resolution for the survivors, Bolan texted back. I'm going to very publicly destroy the Chief 12, Le Loupe Grotte and especially Kiloton.

How much do you have on these groups? Brognola asked.

Building the database, but I'm nearly up to speed with everything about them, Bolan responded. The video makes them out to be far more insane than they truly are.

There were similar rumors that the Tonton Macoutes ate not only bodies, but the souls of their enemies, Brognola interjected. They're building a shield of fear.

Precisely, Bolan answered. I know how effective those are. They were convinced I was an indestructible master of war.

You aren't? Brognola replied.

Serious business now, Hal.

You're not the boogeyman anymore. We've done everything we could to bury that past for you, Brognola explained.

I know secrets have to be kept. But they will fear what I will do to them.

How soon is this going to happen?

There was quiet on the other end. It had been a bit of hubris for Brognola to ask his friend what he was going to do. He'd been on hand for Bolan blitzes across the globe over the years, and had the layout of his general tactics.

Come dusk, maybe an hour or two of observation and reconnaissance, the Executioner would slip in and fire the opening shots in his crusade. Whatever he planned, it was going to be big, and despite how random and messy it would appear, it would be planned down to the millisecond so that not a single innocent bystander would be harmed in the conflagration.

When it came to precision strikes, no laser-guided munition had a single edge on the one-man army known as Mack Bolan.

Godspeed, Brognola signed off.

I hope that's fast enough, Bolan returned, disappearing into the electronic ether.

Brognola knew where that fatalistic thought came from.

The gang had engaged in mass murder, a violent assault that hadn't been seen since the days of the Wild West and violent outlaw gangs attacking small towns. These days, the firepower was even more ferocious, and explosives had the punch to turn buildings into splinters from three hundred yards away. If the Executioner stumbled once, there would be dozens dead.

He had to move in swiftly, strike exactly as hard as necessary, and be out of the way before the police and the federal task force assembled to deal with this prison break came rushing in. Bolan wouldn't shoot at an officer of the law, especially if he was doing his job in protecting the city, let alone if he was simply corrupt.

That solid-rock standing kept Bolan from sliding down a slippery slope where the death of innocents could be balanced against his mission. If it came to the point where he skidded on that moral footing, Bolan and Brognola both knew that the Executioner could become a far worse menace than the enemies he battled.

Bolan's calling was not only to punish and execute the guilty, but to protect the innocent.

Brognola sent a silent prayer, as usual, to his friend, hoping that his dance on the razor's edge didn't cut him this time.

3

Night fell upon the small home on the outskirts of Miami in a suburb known as El Portal. It abutted the neighborhood known as Little Haiti, and was also the home of Officer Elizabeta Montoya. The home was quiet, dark. It had been abandoned for several days, thanks to the policewoman's disappearance, the children taken in by relatives.

The scene had a strange, eerie sense that Bolan could feel. He smelled the rot of death, and the hard, tingling edge of violence made his nerves go on full alert. The warrior opened the back door after running his knife through some crime scene tape. Inside he saw the mess that had been the kitchen. He could readily see the violence of what had happened. Sure, he'd gotten digital photographs from the Miami-Dade crime scene documentation division, but he wanted to get a feel for it.

Carl Lyons, Bolan's longtime friend and ally, had told him that the instincts of an investigator could discover more than just what was shown on a piece of glossy paper or a monitor. The ex-cop was correct, as usual. He was sure that detectives could make out that the entry had been calm. The door latch wasn't broken, kicked in against a dead-bolt latch. It had been opened by someone inside.

Further looking at the door and its frame showed that Montoya may not have had much money, but she had managed to affix the door with good, steel hinges and strong wood for the jamb. Hammering down this door would require more than even a two-man ram. The door, however, looked as if it had been assailed with one or two raps with a length of heavy iron. Just to keep up an appearance.

Things were strewed around, but there was no sign of exactly where the violence would have been. Everything that hadn't been picked up by the crime scene cleaners looked as if it had merely been swept off the counters. Bolan's eyes narrowed as he looked around.

Montoya had disappeared while her children were out.

Haitian drug gang members didn't give a damn about killing a cop and small children. They'd have taken the kids, too.

Bolan hated to think of that, but he knew that there was something to this line of thought. She was given up, but as a means of a controlled sacrifice. He consulted his files once more, turning to what he had gathered about Montoya. He had to check her partners, her coworkers, even rivals if necessary.

This wasn't to say that Montoya had been taken willingly.

Other things entered the twisted equation. This suburb was close to Little Haiti, which meant that Le Loupe Grotte's ethnic home in Miami was within spitting distance.

Bolan set his jaw. Brognola would be hard at work, coordinating events inside West Palm Beach, so law enforcement was going to be busy in that city on this night. People would be traveling in from other parts of the country, shoring up the odds, trying to assemble a task force.

That would give the Executioner a little bit of time. And with that, he could take the disappearance of Montoya and tie it into why two maniacs decided to engage in an apocalyptic attack on West Palm's courthouse.

He returned to his car and headed for an address mentioned three or four times in Montoya's file. It was in Little Haiti, and the way the Executioner's instincts tingled, he was glad that he'd brought the Honey Badger for some close-quarter mayhem, if necessary.

Driving the block, Bolan reviewed the address in his mind. This place had been the home of Ian Tonne's girlfriend, now missing. Montoya, alongside her partner, Tony Nappico, had been called there on three occasions to deal with domestic disturbances. On his first pass, Bolan made out someone inside the small, one-floor, bar-windowed residence. The house was built along the lines of low-cost, low-rent-district prefabricated housing. There was a postage stamp's worth of front yard that was fenced in by chain-link, with likely a similar small amount out back. There were signs that there had once been a garage, but all that remained was a burned-down wreckage of the shack.

Bolan frowned as he took a second pass. According to the report that Montoya filed, Tonne had set the garage on fire when she and her partner arrived for the second of the domestic disturbances. Tonne's girlfriend, Selena Martinique, had been trying to call attention to the burning building, pushing Montoya toward it. In the confusion, nothing was resolved except for Tonne's promise to "behave."

The official report showed redactions and a reprimand from the Dade County prosecutor.

Finally, Bolan parked three blocks away from the house.

Tonne's act of arson wasn't surprising for a domestic disturbance. Police hated those calls, because the heightened tensions and anger often led to self-destructive acts of mayhem. However, the redactions pointed to a bit of prosecutory reprimand. Montoya may have accidentally sabotaged a long-standing case by even looking at what had been left behind in the garage.

With the selective-fire Beretta nestled, suppressor attached, in his shoulder holster, Bolan was able to go EVA with only a dark blue and white flower-patterned shirt to disguise his armed status. A jacket would have been telling, even on a relatively cool Florida evening. The bulky shirt did much to hide the Beretta, and its tails hung low enough to obscure the butt of his .44 Magnum Desert Eagle. To disguise the Honey Badger, he'd placed it in the bottom of a paper grocery bag, clutching it to his side. One yank, and he'd have the compact weapon out, along with the four extra magazines sheathed in its sling.

He'd downloaded the pistol with its 220-grain subsonic rounds, each carrying a massive punch, yet not containing so much powder that it would produce a blinding fireball or deafening muzzle blast. He didn't intend to make a hard contact, not yet. But there were no guarantees that he wouldn't end up pitched into deadly combat in the next few minutes.

Striding down the sidewalk, grocery bag in place, folded over at the top so he could use the folded, crumpled paper as a handle, Bolan didn't look out of place. Sure, he was big and tall, but his skin was tanned enough to pass for a Mexican, and just to be certain, he had put in brown contact lenses to disguise his piercing blue gaze. The breathable lenses didn't do much to his vision, and were soft, so to be quite comfortable, minimizing his distractions in case of violence.

Even so, Bolan was alone, without backup. Despite being more heavily armed than a SWAT team, he was in the middle of a residential neighborhood, which would limit his ability to return fire, though the Haitian gang members would have no such restriction or moral compunction about gunning down innocents several houses away.

Every single shot the Executioner fired had to be on target, or he didn't dare loose a bullet.

That was fine with Bolan. He'd spent his whole adult life fighting his War Everlasting. He never fired without being sure of his target, or the safety consequences of a bullet penetrating through or missing the enemy altogether. His mind was ablaze with the angles on other houses, and where to aim to get the most out of hard backstops like vehicles or cement lamppost bases.

And if worse came to worst, Bolan had adjusted his Desert Eagle's gas system to operate with Glaser Safety rounds meant for the .44 Magnum. The rounds were expensive, but the benefits of being able to shoot without concern about penetrating a window and hitting a homeowner were incalculable. Bolan wasn't giving anything up, either. The hypervelocity slug hit with more than 770 foot-pounds of energy.

Bolan reached the house, then walked to the garage's remains. Charred wood and other detritus were strewed across the concrete foundation of the destroyed structure. He pushed planks around with the tip of his combat boot, using a red-filtered LED flashlight to illuminate the ground. The red filter would keep him from being seen and thus prevent others from noticing he was snooping.

An engine rumbled on the street, even as his boot sole scratched a seam in the concrete. It wasn't a crack—it was too straight, too even. Bolan cast a glance toward the rumbling engine and noticed a dark SUV pulling to a stop across the street. He killed the LED flashlight, pocketing it, but if they had noticed him, it was like closing the barn door after the horse ran away.

The seam had to have been to a trap door. Florida wasn't known for its properties with basements, but the yard and driveway were fresh and new, despite the fire damage to the garage.

It didn't make sense for Tonne not to have cleared away the wreckage if he was that interested in a good-looking piece of property. However, it was perfect for making people disinterested in a closer look at the floor.

While the driveway and lawn were being done, it wouldn't have taken much to isolate some land and install a small compartment beneath the garage foundation.

That was what Montoya had discovered.

Bolan's eyes narrowed. This structure looked very familiar, and then he had it. It resembled the bolt-hole Saddam Hussein had been discovered in. While Kilo and Tonne had been presumed dead, no one would have thought to look underneath a slab of concrete at his girlfriend's old home. Especially not when there had been several reports of domestic disturbance there.

Why hide where you constantly get into conflict? would be the reasoning that made this a hideout.

He pulled out his Combat PDA, ears peeled, senses alert for movement in and around the dark SUV parked across the street. After idling for a moment, it finally killed its engine, but no doors opened. He sent off a quick message to Stony Man Farm to figure out when Tonne had made the renovations, and how far along the federal case against the Chief Dozen had been.

Deep in his heart, though, Bolan knew the time lines would match up to the ending days of Kiloton's first reign of terror.

Bolan pocketed the CPDA once more, then turned and looked directly at the SUV. In the darkness, his attuned eyes made out that the driver's-side window was open, and a burly brute with a leonine mane of hair twisted into dreadlocks sat, staring at him. He was backlit by another who was puffing on a cigarette.

There was no doubt. The men in the truck were interested in him because he showed an interest in the garage. Bolan held his ground, however. If they were policemen, he'd spark a gunfight and kill good men trying to do their job, the same task he had, fighting the savages who twisted their Haitian heritage and religious beliefs into a justification for wanton murder.

Of course, waiting for them to give him some trouble meant that he would be standing as a helpless target should they suddenly decide to open fire. Bolan began walking down the driveway, cutting a little across the lawn to continue on toward the sidewalk.

"Hey, man!" the driver shouted in a voice as deep and rumbly as his mass of hair made him look lionlike. "What's it your business looking there?"

"Saw somethin' run into the junk," Bolan returned, affecting a Hispanic accent. "Didn't mean no harm. Whose was this place? A friend's?"

"Well, you're not a redneck, so it couldn't have been a possum. You chicos don't eat roadkill," the grumbling voice said.

"I answered one of your questions." Bolan spoke up. "How about answering one of mine?"

There was movement. Someone else must have gotten out of the SUV before it came to a stop, maybe even a block back as they'd noticed the tall, unknown man. Bolan could pass for Hispanic, but he was still in Little Haiti, where even darker skin was the norm, and not being white was no guarantee of safety. Not that the Executioner required a guarantee of his own personal safety.

He pretended not to notice the newcomer flanking him. There

was something different about the man's vibe, and his build was smaller, more traditionally Hispanic.

"Miami PD?" Bolan asked, dropping his accent.

"What makes you think that?" the booming voice asked.

"Because Le Loupe Grotte would have put a bullet in the back of my head about now," Bolan answered. He set down his grocery bag, then opened his shirt to reveal his armament and the Justice Department badge. "Also, Haitians don't work closely with *Cubanos*."

"How do we know that badge is real?" the man flanking him asked. "Besides, those don't look like cop guns."

Bolan turned his head toward the newcomer. He tossed the badge wallet over. "Hard to look like a cop when you're carrying PD-issue USPs. You whip out a Desert Eagle, people know you're not a lawman."

"Except for you," the big man said, getting out of the SUV. Bolan could see a long, gleaming silver SIG-Sauer pistol with an extended barrel in his hamlike fist. "And…maybe me."

"If you want to know what I was looking at…" Bolan began.

"Not before we check out this ID," the smaller Cuban said.

The badge was real, and if someone looked at it, it would identify him as Special Agent Matthew Cooper. It would take someone with supernatural senses to penetrate the impermeable smell test associated with the badge. This was the identity that got folded away, hidden beneath another identity when he was on an officially sanctioned Sensitive Operations Group mission. Anyone who asked what Cooper was doing presently would find that he was off duty by following the contact and bona fides attached to the badge. It was the closest thing to a Stony Man cover identity as he had with him. Everything else was straight out of the Executioner's pocket, an amassing of technology, information and equipment he assembled under his own wits and power.

The big Haitian glared at his partner for a moment. "The man has a submachine gun in his paper sack, and he doesn't use it, and you're wondering if he's real?"

The Cuban looked down at the credentials, then at Bolan, then at the paper bag. Curiosity got the better of the cop and he opened the bag, giving a low whistle as he looked at the weapon within. As opposed to other Honey Badgers that were in the testing stages, this one was solid, nonreflective black. There was hardly a shiny surface on the compact machine pistol, only the Aimpoint scope's glass showing the slightest of gleams.

"I guess you'd have the papers for this little thing?" the Cuban cop asked.

Bolan nodded.

The cop looked down at the badge wallet once more. Special agent was obvious, though Bolan's dress and demeanor belied an agent who was "on duty." "You're not bullying us, so I'm doubting you're FBI. But why look a gift horse in the mouth?" He handed the wallet back. "I'm Jeff Perez. That mountain there is Carl Montenegro."

"Black mountain. Looks like an apt name," Bolan mused.

Montenegro grinned. "Big people are pretty common in my family."

"That was a good Haitian accent you pulled," Bolan said.

"You, too…"

Bolan answered with the name on the badge. "Matt Cooper. So what are you two?"

"Metro-Dade County," Montenegro said as they walked back to the charred remains of the garage. "And you're Justice Department."

Bolan nodded. "Undercover."

"You came here because you recognized Montoya's relationship to Ian Tonne," Perez said. He ran his thumb across his chin, the scratch of his stubble sounding a bit like a match lighting. "And figured there was something in the garage floor."

"You did, too?" Bolan asked.

"Once we caught a whiff that she was tortured to death on a video made by Kiloton," Montenegro said, "we came by, hoping to see someone."

"You found me," Bolan answered.

Montenegro shrugged. "That's the shame. We wanted one of the Haitians."

Bolan knelt to the garage floor and pulled his automatic knife when Montenegro cleared his throat, excused himself, and took out a chisel-tipped "rescue knife." The thing had cutting and sawing edges, and a beveled front edge that could be used as a crowbar. It slipped into the seam and within a moment the concrete slab rose enough for the three men to move it aside.

Inside, the funk of two men hiding out was unmistakable. As Perez was the smallest of the trio, he slid through the opening, but even his broad shoulders were a tight fit.

Underneath, he found just what Bolan had suspected. A cramped little den, large enough for two men to secret themselves. Perez also called out that he saw a tunnel leading in the direction of the house. Of course there would be a means to safer passage. There was no way anyone was scurrying out of that bolt-hole quickly.

Now Bolan knew why Montoya had been the first victim of Kilo and Tonne.

But there were more questions.

Bolan spoke solemnly. "So what happened to Tony Nappico and Selena Martinique?"

ANTHONY NAPPICO LET THE tequila bottle topple sideways as he released its neck too soon. Bleary-eyed, head pounding, his mouth was dry as a bone.

He didn't worry about wasting alcohol. The bottle was empty, as empty as his soul felt. He wasn't using a shot glass—he had been draining the liquor straight from the neck. This had been his fifth in as many days, and he was certain that he was on the fast track to liver failure.

The cop would have eaten a gun, but liver failure was much more easily paid off than suicide. Nappico felt that he was the worst human being on the planet, but his death benefits would have been more than enough to make certain his estranged wife and children wouldn't starve.

There was a rap at the door and Nappico looked at the blurred red letters on his clock. It was getting close to eleven at night. Who would want to bother him at this time?

Unless it was Emile or Ian.

He fumbled for the Heckler & Koch USP .40 he kept under his pillow, then staggered to the door. Along the way, he kicked empty cans and bottles drained of cheap beer. If anyone came in here, they would have thought that a spring break party had hit the little trailer. This was all his own doing.

Montoya's brown eyes looked, agonized, into his own every time he blinked. No amount of alcohol would have been able to shunt that aside. But he tried. And he failed miserably.

Nappico opened the door and saw two of the biggest men he'd ever seen. A stiff arm lashed out and rammed him in the throat, squeezing and pushing him back into the darkness of the trailer.

"Trying to drink yourself to death?" the man, a deeply tanned white, asked as he looked around.

"Get the fuck out of my house!"

The white man glared, staring deep into his eyes. Since Bolan had removed his contact lenses, the drunken cop was gazing into two icy orbs that chilled his soul. Nappico's pistol was gone, and he didn't remember dropping it. His index finger hurt, strained and pulled by a savage twist he hadn't seen.

Nappico was unarmed with two brutes at his door.

"Trying to die?" Bolan asked him, leaning in close.

Nappico looked down at his hand, with its sprained index finger. He noticed that his H&K USP was now locked in his assailant's fist. "What is it to you?"

"So why did you give up your partner?" a mountain of a man, this one black, asked from behind the blue-eyed warrior.

"So her kids and my kids could grow up," Nappico snarled. "Pull the trigger. You shoot me, it won't be suicide."

"So those two maniacs promised not to murder your families," Bolan said, easing up on the pressure. Nappico was glad he had been pushed against his kitchenette counter. He couldn't have stood on his own.

Nappico nodded. "I have to die, too. Otherwise…"

A sharp slap focused the cop's mind on a single flare of anger, burning through the haze of drunkenness and self-loathing.

He felt the USP being stuffed back into his waistband and was unresisting as he was carted over to the bed. It was then that he saw Perez, dwarfed and lost amid the huge presences of Bolan and Montenegro. He actually could recognize Perez. They'd worked together on a task force or two.

"How could you do this to her?" Perez asked.

Bleary, blurry, Nappico didn't have anything to say.

But a photo, a snapshot of a happier time, where Nappico and his family were posing together with Montoya and her kids and sister, the affection glowing on that image, was all that was necessary.

"You gonna let two Haitian enforcers get their hands on the children?" Nappico asked.

Bolan spoke up. "No sane man would."

Perez shot the man a dirty look.

"I've lost friends to torture artists like those two," Bolan added in explanation. "Bad enough to have an adult you know and love slaughtered like that. I couldn't bear to see kids done that way."

"You understand?" Nappico asked.

Bolan looked at him for a moment, a brief instance that there might be some sympathy, some warmth in the warrior's eyes. Then that brutal cold returned. Nappico, already reeling with doubt and remorse, felt as if he'd been slapped hard across the face. His thumb traced the grenade-pattern checkering on the bottom of his USP's grip. No, he didn't entertain any thoughts about shooting it out. Though he was tempted to put the muzzle to the side of his head and blast his brains across the wall.

The thing was, Bolan's glare was riveting. He couldn't move, couldn't act on his wish to end all of this suffering with a pull of the trigger.

"Why not tell the prosecutor's office?" Bolan asked. "Why not look for protective custody?"

Nappico's head drooped. "Shoot me. Get it over with."

"You're not going to be that lucky," Montenegro told him. "We need to talk."

Nappico shuddered at that statement. "So, you'll let them kill my kids and ex?"

"No one else is going to die because of you," Perez told him.

Bolan cut him off. "No. That's a lie."

Again, the angry look.

"Emile Kilo and Ian Tonne are going to die because of him," Bolan explained. "Talk to me."

"We thought you were Justice," Montenegro said.

Bolan narrowed his eyes. "There are different kinds of justice. Besides, I don't think the two of you will have jurisdiction down in West Palm."

"Damn it," Perez muttered. "She was one of us. We're going to let this ass slide because…"

Bolan's glare drowned Perez out. "He's not going to slide."

"I'm in no condition to help. And what about the asshole watching me?" Nappico asked.

"Cooper took care of that," Montenegro said. "Saw him when we rolled up, and he took the man down. Shame we didn't shoot him."

"You're going to accommodate this kind of vigilante bullshit?" Perez asked. "We're cops!"

"You heard what happened at the West Palm courthouse this morning," Montenegro answered. "Montoya's not the only dead badge today."

Perez grimaced. "I took a vow to uphold the law."

Nappico looked at Perez. He had seen the county deputy talking a lot with Montoya. She had been tight-lipped, but even through his current haze, he could tell that there were feelings for the woman. Strong feelings. He could tell that she'd returned them. "Look, I'm sorry…"

Perez leaned in closer. "I want nothing more than to skin you alive. But instead, I'm going to make sure the law lands on you so hard—"

"He's going to work with me," Bolan interjected.

"What the hell are you talking about?" Montenegro asked. "We're the ones who helped you find where Kiloton had been hiding out."

"I can't ask you two to join me," Bolan said. "Not any further than this. We came here to get some answers, and we got them. You can do whatever you want with this information. I'm going on to West Palm."

Nappico frowned. "I just want to keep my family safe."

"You will. This place will burn down," Bolan said. "The Haitian will wake up, see the flames, and figure that you're dead. That will give us a night, maybe two, considering Le Loupe Grotte is busy with other things."

"Like running from all the law coming down to West Palm," Montenegro said. "I'm good and pissed, and want to do something about Montoya."

Nappico could read the concern for Perez in the strain of Montenegro's voice.

"You said you can't ask them," Nappico slurred.

"Right now, you'll be a liability to me as drunk as you are. But you've got information in your head," Bolan said. "And your life looks over. It hangs on you. Do you want to go out in self-destruction, or go out trying to save lives and stop killers?"

Nappico wanted to reach for the H&K USP in his waistband. Bolan's words, however, cut through the alcohol haze. No, he couldn't fight, but he did have names, dates, locations. "Let them finish me off."

The Executioner turned to Perez and Montenegro. "If you want to do something to pull Kilo or Tonne's fangs, then go get his family."

Perez raised his hand. "I'll do it. And check on Liz's kids."

There was a pause. "What about Tonne? He's at work down in West Palm."

"They've got support here," Montenegro mentioned. "Hell, they've been hiding at Martinique's house. There's got to be some command structure here."

Bolan handed over a card to Montenegro. "If you find anything about it, call him. You two don't kick down any doors by yourself. This man will get you support, everything from SWAT to helicopters."

The two men looked at the small slip of paper.

Perez spoke first in a low whistle. "He's been asking for help from our department and Miami PD...."

"Your boss?" Montenegro asked.

"My friend. I don't work for him, and I'm not working *with* him on this foray," Bolan said.

The two Metro Dade detectives looked at him askance.

"Do as you say, not as you do," Perez concluded.

"I'm not being hypocritical, Jeff," Bolan said. "I've long since consigned myself to a violent end, and working just outside of the law. I'll suffer the consequences. No one else."

"Except for me," Nappico added. He waved to his mess of bottles and cans. "But then, I'm a dead man anyway."

"We both are," Bolan whispered. "Let's ask Kilo, Tonne and their friends to join us."

4

The drive to West Palm Beach was a fast one, especially since Bolan's borrowed car was a 470 horsepower hunk of street-legal muscle. As the Dodge Challenger growled and accelerated down the road, Tony Nappico sucked on a thermos full of coffee to wash the cobwebs out of his brain. He still wasn't going to be in fighting trim for hours, but the coffee and his guilt had loosened his tongue easily.

With the information Bolan was getting out of the man, the warrior felt both a flush of compassion and simultaneous impatience with Nappico.

The event that had inspired Nappico to go to Montoya's house and take her to the two murderous Haitian thugs was the delivery of an envelope containing head-shot photographs of his own and Montoya's children. Each of them was circled in bloody red and crossed out.

The message was grim and ominous.

"She didn't put up a fight," Nappico confessed. "She saw her babies in those pics, and she came with me. If I could have, I'd have shot her, made the end come quickly. They sent me a preview."

"That's why you didn't shoot yourself," Bolan said. The 392-cubic-inch engine rumbled louder as he accelerated, slipping between a pair of semis that were on the road ahead. He'd dallied enough in Miami and its suburb of El Portal. He'd gathered major information, but presently Bolan was cutting his

lead against the assembled forces of Florida and federal law enforcement in his hunt for the murderous Chief Dozen escapees.

Bolan's Florida contact had given him the Dodge because
its backseat had the room to stuff in a prisoner or to stow away
his lighter small arms. The warrior would be out of luck if he
were intending to carry along something like a full-length M-82
.50-caliber anti-matériel rifle, but he could fit a bull-pup Barrett
M-95, which was only 45 inches in length. As both the Smith
& Wesson MP-15 in .300 Blackout and the Honey Badger were
far more compact, the room was quite generous.

The dashboard had a multimedia information center, including a large liquid-crystal screen for a built-in GPS. Bolan had
plugged his Combat PDA into its Firewire jack, synchronizing
the car's data to his own files, allowing for the Dodge to be a
mobile intelligence command center, if necessary. The electronic brain inside the muscle car, combined with the high-
tech design of Hermann Schwarz, did everything his early War
Wagon could only dream of doing, with only a fraction of the
space.

Though, to be fair, the War Wagon was also Bolan's home
on the road, had room for his gunsmithing and hand-loading for
the mighty .44 Auto Mag, and had a built-in, disguised, laser-
guided rocket launcher. The Dodge didn't have an armorer's
bench, and its driver's seat was a poor substitute for a bed, even
disregarding the necessity for Bolan to "rock a rocket launcher"
built into the snarling Challenger.

Nappico slumped low in his seat, his eyes barely over the bottom of the passenger-side window. His black hair was a matted,
sweaty mess, and his face was sallow and shrunken.

"Keep drinking the water," Bolan said. "You've dehydrated
yourself too much from the booze bender you've been on."

Nappico turned. "Why are you giving me a chance?"

Bolan remained silent, concentrating on his driving as he
visualized his angle of attack into West Palm. He fought the
temptation to coddle the broken cop next to him. Given his
druthers, Bolan would have found a different means of restor-

ing the man's faith in himself. Drinking himself into destruction, Nappico had been digging his grave for days. Bolan was certain that there were letters sent out, implicating himself in the destruction of his partner and friend.

Even if there wasn't, as if this night there were two more people who knew what he had done.

Nappico intruded again. "Cooper?"

"I'm giving you a chance because you want one," Bolan said. "You were given an impossible choice."

Nappico looked down.

"No. I can't tell you that you did the right thing," Bolan continued. "I know you wanted to. You took the lesser evil. But even that…"

"You wouldn't have handed her over," Nappico said.

Bolan shifted, giving himself some extra traction as he switched lanes, spearing the Challenger past a wolf pack of cars cruising along at around 70 miles an hour. The multimedia screen was quiet. There was a radar detector in the system, and it was looking for speed zones.

The last thing that Bolan needed was to encounter the Florida Highway Patrol by going too fast. At this time of night, though, the highway was relatively clear. He was certain the state police would be interested in other things in the wake of the bloody Chief Dozen attack and escape.

He drove to make time, but not recklessly.

"Truth told, I don't have people to turn over," Bolan told him. "I know what a wrecked life feels like."

Nappico looked down.

"You still have a thread of a chance," Bolan said. "I don't know if it will be enough, but I don't want another family destroyed like Montoya's."

"Thank you," Nappico whispered.

Bolan frowned. He was on a fine line here. He didn't want Nappico totally despondent, but he also needed the man motivated and unafraid of personal consequences. Even if they survived this, even if they managed to clear Nappico publicly, the man had too much emotional trauma to be worth much after this event. He'd carry the memory of his betrayal, a guilt eating at him like a cancer, the rest of his days, no matter what he did.

Someday, Nappico—no matter how much he confessed, how much he moralized it—would still want to die. He'd end up in a grave either due to consequences of his own pain or by the simple action of suicide.

And that ate at Bolan. The only peace the cop could find would be in a grave, but there was no part of the Executioner, the man also known as Sergeant Mercy, that would let such a person die like that. He couldn't provide the release of death, either. It simply wasn't part of his morality. And yet, there was nothing to salve that kind of wound.

Instead of agonizing over the impossible, Bolan kept his mind, and his eyes, on the road ahead.

Things were going to get even bloodier.

ZOE SIFUENTES DIDN'T HAVE the strength to snarl in disdain as she was given a microphone and a camera was turned on her. She'd been giving her testimony for the past ten hours to cops and Feds who came in looking for more information about Emile Kilo and his conversation with her. Her stomach still churned as she remembered the horrors on the DVD given to her. She wanted to go to sleep—no, go into a dreamless coma. If she closed her eyes, she saw the horrible mutilation that Elizabeta Montoya endured before she'd died at the hands of the two killers.

"Latest estimates of the death toll are twelve officers and federal agents dead, and another fifteen citizens, among them members of this station's news team. The injured haven't been confirmably tabulated, but there are at least sixty suffering from various wounds," Zoe said. She was bleary, and it was a wonder that she could keep her eyes open.

She looked at the camera. "Jacobs, you were Rivera's friend. You can't push the camera aside for one minute?"

Jacobs tilted his head out from behind the viewfinder. "Zoe, this is big news. The biggest news in the country right now. If we're not doing this, someone else will pick up the scraps."

Zoe pushed some hair out of her face. The back of her hand brushed the stinging lacerations across her forehead, and she winced at the touch. "I don't feel so good."

"Just take a few breaths…" Jacobs said.

Then, in her earphone and his, the voice of the producer back at the station bellowed. "This is live! Stop bitching, you two!"

"I'm not bitching, you soulless ghoul," Zoe growled into the microphone as she stumbled to the ground. "I'm sorry, but our producer on this segment is currently griping that I'm not reporting like a professional. I humbly submit to that asshole that he should try giving a shit about a broadcast after he'd been bombed!"

With that, she let the microphone tumble from her fingers, then struggled to her feet. To his credit, Jacobs set down the camera and helped her to her feet. She didn't have much balance, but once she built up some momentum, she was able to walk without his guidance.

"Don't get fired," Zoe told him. "Go back to the camera."

"And film what? We've got enough footage of carnage and cops setting up shop to fill twenty hours without repeat," Jacobs said. "You're in a world of hurt right now."

"Miss Sifuentes?" a deep voice asked. The two stopped and looked to see a burly, gray-haired man in a suit. Around his neck, he wore a chain with a leather badge holder, and in the breast pocket of his jacket, a folded ID proclaimed him Harold Brognola of the Justice Department. The Fed was flanked by a pair of men wearing dark glasses and black clothing. Both had powerful-looking compact weapons slung over their shoulders.

"What now?" Zoe asked.

"I'm not going to interrogate you again," Brognola said. "I'm more concerned with your safety."

Zoe blinked. "My safety?"

"You were present at the 'death' of these two men," Brognola stated. "We have reason to believe that the woman in that video you were given also had dealings with those two in the past."

"The police woman," Zoe repeated. "Who are these two?" the reporter said, pointing to the two armed men.

"Justice Department Marshals, Deputies Johnson and Johnson," Brognola intoned. "I'm giving them to you for your protection."

"'Protection,'" Zoe parroted. It was then that she realized that she was echoing what he said. She shook her head. "You think he'll come after me?"

"You were the one who broadcast their alleged deaths. They wanted you to send a message," Brognola stated. "And now that you're done, you are just a reminder of what was their lowest point. They will come after you and kill you."

"So these are my personal bodyguards?" Zoe asked, looking at the pair. One of them was a mulatto, a man with a mixture of features that hinted at a Middle Eastern background, especially since he had an African American nose but the straight, thick hair of an Arab. The other was a stocky, shorter man wearing a knit cap, from under which blond hairs poked. "Johnson and Johnson, eh?"

"We're a gentle, no-tears formula," the mulatto Johnson said with a warm, friendly smirk.

The cap-wearing one looked at his friend. "We're not doing the no-relation bit anymore?"

"That ran its course," the taller man told him. "Besides, like it or not, we are brothers."

The stocky guard smiled.

"Kind of a goofy pair," Zoe said to Brognola.

"Don't worry about them. That's their mouths in idle," Brognola said. "When the shit hits the fan, they're all professional."

Zoe had to admit that Brognola had a point. For all their banter, their eyes were constantly scanning the area. Though they had automatic weapons, they kept the muzzles aimed at the ground, so as not to cross any other people around them, a violation of one of the first four tenets of firearms safety. Zoe had covered enough police and attended enough training seminars to know that these two were almost unconsciously aware of their surroundings, their aspect and their positions. "Got real names?"

"Call me Dave," the short one said.

"I'm Lando," the taller one added.

The short one shook his head. "That pirate guy ruined a perfectly good name."

The taller one smiled. "Ruined? I'm flippin' Lando, now."

"That's why you call your car the Falcon?" Dave asked. He shook his head again. "I'm getting slow in my old age."

"Too much of that BBC crap rots your brains," Lando said with a wink.

Brognola shrugged. "You get protection with a side order of running jokes."

Zoe chuckled. "I've had worse babysitters."

"Don't let her die," Brognola scolded the pair, but Zoe could tell that his tone was only gentle ribbing.

"We've got her, boss," Lando said. Dave echoed with a smart salute.

"You think he's going to make a move tonight?" she asked.

"We're not taking any chances. Come with us, ma'am," Dave told her. "This place is too open."

With that, they relieved Jacobs of his burden of helping her walk along.

"Stay safe," Jacobs called to her.

After the brutal horrors she'd seen this morning, Zoe didn't believe that there were any safe places left in the world.

IT WOULD BE SAFER for Nappico in the Challenger, Bolan determined, but that was only a matter of relative nature. West Palm Beach was ground zero for a spasm of violence and destruction that had remained quiet since the initial eruption earlier in the morning. The warrior looked over the hotel as he searched for which rooms were inhabited and which were empty.

One glance at the pool, unlit, and stinking of moss and decay, and Bolan knew that business had long ago passed over this place. Though the Gulf had recovered its tourism business, West Palm was on the other side of the isthmus that made up the majority of Florida's land area. The city itself was in fairly good condition, all things considered, and tourist money was keeping the coffers filled in most areas.

However, Bolan knew that this hotel, while it still paid its utilities, was nothing more than a front. It wasn't a place for guests, but more of a barracks for Haitian soldiers and a prison block for hostages. The prosecution's documentation laid out that there had been three torture-murders, each identical in nature to Montoya's demise.

Unfortunately, this information was not allowed into the court records, the defense lawyers having convinced the bench that the run-down hotel and the Chief Dozen's involvement were all achieved through an unwarranted search. "Fruit of the poison vine," was what it was referred to in legalese, but if there was one thing the Executioner could stomach about these cases, it was that legally deadly morsel. He could eat from that cornucopia for days, and strengthen himself in regard to hitting his enemy where they felt they were the strongest.

Bolan's previous stops had been investigation only, despite the presence of the Honey Badger in the grocery bag back in Little Haiti. But this time the compact .300-caliber weapon was on a sling around his neck, six spare magazines in a drop pouch on his left thigh across from the SWAT holster for his Desert Eagle. The silenced Beretta hung in its shoulder harness, one 20-round magazine in place, balanced by two more sticks with the same capacity on the other side of his torso. All told, he had 267 rounds of ammunition with him. He also had a trio of flash-bang stun grenades, two combat blades, a knuckle duster and a polymer wire garrotte on hand.

This was the Executioner in urban blitz mode. He was here to hit hard, find the missing Selena Martinique, and git. The moment he got what he needed, he was leaving behind a message in no uncertain terms.

Kiloton had declared war, but the forces of law and order had their own weapon of mass destruction, a one-man army hell-bent on avenging the thirty plus murdered so far on this rampage. They wouldn't know that it was the same Executioner who had struck the Florida peninsula to battle organized crime, to hurl Cuban-backed terrorists or expatriate zealots off American shores. There would be no one to call this the Bolan Blitz, but the results would be the same.

Dead, armed thugs, smashed and destroyed in the wake of one man's attack. Supposedly superior odds would fall before the precision violence, applied with scalpel-sharp keenness.

He'd made three orbits around the hotel, scanning within, watching for guards and timing their patterns. There were four guards, each of varying build, and they were grim and determined-looking. He made out several weapons among them. Two had sawed-off shotguns, while the other two had cheap, basement-built Ingram MAC-11s, judging by how visible their welding seams appeared on his night-vision binoculars.

They looked quite prepared to open fire on anyone coming close. Several rooms were occupied, he counted. He could see rubbish strewed off to the sides of doors, swept aside as residents exited and entered. He didn't want to set himself to an exact number as he didn't want to underestimate the enemy odds, but given the nature of the Haitian gang members, it would be unlikely that more than two would share a hotel room. They were too "manly" and "macho" to stomach the thought of sharing even a queen-size bed with another male.

There might also be one prisoner in the hotel, given that there was yet another sentry, this one armed with a long rifle, standing at a door. The shoulder-arm resembled an SKS, except this one had been converted to hold a 30-round AK-47-style magazine. He knew some Eastern European designers had replaced the integral box magazine with a removable system to provide commonality with other Warsaw Pact rifles, and he knew that the SKS was much more accurate than the AK it preceded. Bolan was familiar with the AK-47 and its descendants, but its barrel tended to flex, a built-in feature that allowed the rifle to spread its autofire. Taking time between single shots allowed it to be intrinsically accurate, but on fully automatic it would clear a room with a long, ragged burst that could zip targets from crotch to throat. The SKS didn't flex like that, and could put its rounds into cloverleaf patterns, the bullets touching on a paper target at under fifty feet.

Bolan knew that the .300 AAC Honey Badger he carried was designed to duplicate the exact ballistic of the rounds that the AK-47 and SKS fired, the only difference being that its cartridges were shaped to fit into the straighter M-16 and M-4 magazines of the Western powers. The Executioner had tested the Badger side-by-side with an AK, and both produced identical channels of massive tissue destruction in sides of beef. One mistake and the Executioner would have his innards churned into a bloody froth.

On the other hand, his enemies would suffer the same horrendous wounds if they were caught in his sights. As always, Bolan's life would depend on split-second reactions and skillful aim.

Bolan closed in on one of the shotgunners walking perimeter around the hotel. As the fence was actually wrought-iron bars, not chain-link, he made no sound as he climbed up and vaulted over the top. His crepe-soled boots were soundless as he landed on the concrete at poolside, legs bent to absorb and cushion his fall, making his arrival inside the hotel compound unnoticed. In this darkened corner, fifteen feet behind the shotgun-toting Haitian, he was just a shadow, making only slightly more sound than one. If the sentry had heard anything, he didn't even flinch at Bolan's landing.

Though his Beretta and the Honey Badger were silenced, at this point in the infiltration, he couldn't risk even the noise of a suppressed weapon. A gunshot was still a gunshot, no matter what was put on the barrel. The weapon that produced the least noise was a carbon filament he took from his belt. The garrotte was pulled taut between its two handles, and Bolan let it slack, turning it to form a loose noose. With a surge, he was behind the Loupe gang member, and he pulled the loop of inelastic line around the man's head. Bolan brought up his knee between the Haitian's shoulder blades as he yanked down hard, snapping the sentry off balance. The fiber didn't stretch, instead cutting into the throat of the guard, chocolate skin parting and bubbling up blood. The sheer pressure of the garrotte wire on his windpipe stifled any attempt to cry for help, but Bolan's powerful hands and arms wrenched harder, collapsing and crushing his larynx. Veins and arteries, unable to resist the unyielding wire, burst.

It only took a few moments, but the guard was dead. He didn't even have a chance to suffocate as blood vessels shredded, hemorrhaging the flow of oxygen to his brain.

Bolan let the man drop to the concrete, winding the bloody fiber and wiping it off on the corpse's shirt. He tucked the weapon away, then pushed the lifeless lump of flesh behind some abandoned poolside deck chairs. It was quick and dirty, a brutal way to kill a man, but this place was where even crueler deaths were staged and executed. Bolan didn't have the time to be fastidious. A second guard would be passing soon on patrol to meet up with the first guard.

He switched to his fighting knife, walking in the same position as the man he'd offed only moments ago. In the dark, his silhouette would be indistinguishable from the first guard, but that brief disguise wouldn't last. Bolan tucked the knife against his forearm, ready to lash out with it before any recognition would flash across the next man's face.

As they closed, the next guard's attention was pointed outward, not toward his comrade. That allowed Bolan to close the distance, hunched and ready to complete the lunge.

"Them cops are gonna get a surprise if they wanna come 'round here, boyah," the guard muttered as he closed with what he assumed was his friend.

Bolan's answer was a swift punch, driving the clip point of his knife through the man's upper chest. A gush of gore spurted out of the wound, and with his bronchial tubes severed by the mighty slash, the Haitian didn't have anything to say. Any attempt to say a word turned into a torrent of bright arterial blood that spilled over his lips.

A hard grab shoved the man's MAC-11 tight against his chest, pinning the Haitian's hand so he couldn't spasm and pull the trigger. Using his knife handle as leverage, Bolan twisted the dying gunman to the ground. A violent wrench of the blade, and ribs cracked audibly. The Executioner pulled the knife back, then kicked the MAC-11 into the pool.

Two guards were down. That didn't mean much, except that Bolan had a clear path into the hotel proper. All of the rooms lead to either the floor next to the pool or to the balcony overlooking it. He made for the stairs at the end of the second-floor walkway. At the far end of the balcony was the door sentry with his rifle.

Bolan checked the Honey Badger and its suppressor. The moment he started shooting, the other guard outside would hear it. He was counting on the hotel room doors, thick enough to ensure privacy, buying him a few moments of quiet shooting. He hoped all he would need would be one shot, which would be even easier to disregard. If not, the hotel would erupt into a gun battle.

Bolan paused halfway on the steps, making certain he was not seen over the landing. The gun was set to single fire, and he triple checked the round in the chamber. One 220-grain Sierra slug would be more than sufficient to stop the Haitian rifleman's heart and drop him.

If it failed, then it was possible that whatever prisoners held behind the door would be killed. He wanted to know what happened to Selena Martinique. It wasn't going to measure much in relation to the lawmen murdered over the past week, but if an innocent woman was still held captive, then Bolan would move heaven and earth to get her back.

Using a pocket mirror, he gauged the position of the Haitian guard. He lined up the angles and knew where he had to pop up. He took a brief moment to align himself, then rose, shoul-

dering the stock of the Honey Badger. The Aimpoint reticule
zeroed on the Loupe Grotte sentry's heart, and he pulled the trigger once. The gunshot was a loud cough, something that could
be heard yards away easily. He was down the hall yet from the
first room on the second floor that seemed to have men inside,
so hopefully the sound would die out quickly.

As it was, the rifleman jerked violently, eyes bulging from
the shock of the impact that tore his heart in two. He stiffened
then toppled, knees gone rubbery. The guard must have been a
professional, because his trigger finger was straight along the
receiver of his gun, no death spasm snapping the hammer to
the primer. He dropped with little more sound than a grunt of
releasing air from dead lungs and the thud of his bulk striking
the ground.

The only trouble with that swift, quiet kill was that it happened just as one of the guards, running ahead of schedule,
stepped into view of the door and the death-stricken rifleman.

"What the hell? Banner?"

Bolan had taken two steps and was already on the walkway
when the Loupe gunman shouted. For all the man knew, the
rifleman could have had a simple heart attack, but the presence
of a white man, dimly illuminated by the balcony's few working bulbs, instantly caught his attention.

The machine pistol rose to cut apart the Executioner as he
was caught, out in the open.

5

The gangster toted a MAC-11 submachine as he patrolled the perimeter of the hard-site when he noticed the tall, powerfully built figure walking on the second-floor balcony. The gunman whipped the compact little chatterbox to bear on the Executioner. Bolan pivoted and fired two shots as fast as he could work the trigger, the first round careening off the railing with a loud clang and ping. The Aimpoint hadn't given him a view of how close his muzzle was to the obstructing steel. The second shot, however, flew true and struck the shooter direct in the upper chest. Rib and clavicle bones were reduced to splinters, and the Haitian was hurled back by his dying reflex. The same death spasm tightened his fist and finger around the gun's trigger, unleashing the rattle of the boxy weapon.

Stealth went to hell as Bolan heard voices behind the doors grumbling into wakefulness.

He was already committed, so he broke into a hard run, racing down the walkway. He charged to the door and brought up his boot to kick just under the knob. Putting all of his two-hundred pounds, plus his extra weight in gear, into the kick, he snapped the door off its hinges.

There was the sound of doors opening behind him as he saw two Haitian men, wearing bloody aprons and face masks, standing over a mangled mass of torn meat.

He was too late for Selena Martinique or whoever that was sprawled out on the table. Twitching limbs betrayed that the horror show leftovers were still alive.

The closest butcher snatched up a huge bone saw and charged toward the Executioner. Bolan didn't give the killer a chance to take more than one step, flicking the Badger to full-auto and releasing a stream of .300-caliber bullets that ripped through the man's sternum, blowing out his heart and spine in one snarling growl. As destructive and flesh-ripping as its namesake, the Honey Badger exploded a mist of blasted tissue from the turkey doctor.

The other slaughterer scrambled and lunged for a pistol on the counter. Bolan triggered the Badger again, bullets chopping the man's arm off as he reached for it. The heavy subsonic slugs had more than sufficient mass to pulverize his elbow joint, subsequent shots severing skin and muscle. The butcher screamed in horror, recoiling from where his limb had been hewed off.

There was movement behind him, and Bolan knew that he didn't have time to deal with the wounded shooter. Luckily, such a violent amputation was likely to leave its victim in shock.

Bolan let the magazine drop from the SMG's well, stuffing a fresh one into place. He didn't want to face an unknown force with less than a full weapon. As he finished his turn toward the door, he spotted five men bursting into view. They were looking all around, confused, but to a man they were armed, shotguns and rifles in their hands. The Executioner wasn't going to take a chance on their reaction time and shouldered the stubby blaster.

On full-auto, the compact Honey Badger rocked at 780 rounds per minute, and a short tug of the trigger swept four slugs through the Haitian closest to the door. Striking with all the speed and power of a standard AK-47, except firing more quickly, Bolan's burst bowled the first of the Loupe's over, the man's shotgun discharging into the ceiling over his head. The close proximity blast of a 12-gauge, without the benefits of hearing protection, deafened and stunned the man immediately to his right. The gunmen hadn't built up enough adrenaline to deal with such a blast.

The next man in the line let his weapon, another SKS, drop to the ground, both hands racing up to his ears to cover them.

The three beyond him spun in reaction to their friend's dying shotgun blast, and saw a sliver of the Executioner's tall frame in the far doorway. One of the Haitians didn't pay any mind to the fact that his coworker was in the way and he triggered the SKS twice, two high-powered 7.62 mm slugs punching through the stunned man's torso. Luckily, the dying guard's fluid mass disrupted the trajectory of those bullets, spattering them against the doorjamb opposite where Bolan had crouched.

Bolan didn't waste any time returning fire. The man with the gut-shot stood gawking at his fellow Loupe member who shot him, providing a small obstacles for the Executioner. So he aimed high and triggered another short burst that mashed the rifleman's face into a bloody crater of sticky blood and chunks of bone.

The wounded Loupe realized that there was trouble behind him, and did the smartest thing in his short life. He folded over, clamped both hands over his belly injuries, and played dead.

As the presently noncombatant no longer formed a solid barrier against subsequent fire, Bolan was free to aim lower, loosing two more shredding bursts that caught the last two men on the walkway at chest height. That final pair went down, no fuss, no muss, the Honey Badger having done its brutal work.

That was the gunmen who were on this floor. There had been more downstairs, including one last extant perimeter guard. Bolan also had two wounded to deal with.

Movement scuffed the floor behind the warrior and he somersaulted beneath the swing of a hook shaped blade large enough to slice a cantaloupe in two. It was the one-armed butcher, and he had recovered enough of his wits to decide to take the fight to Bolan. The Executioner came out of his roll in a low crouch, then launched himself, shoulder tackling the bloody mutilator. Bolan and his opponent crashed into the table where the still living horror lay, and all three slammed to the floor in a jumble.

The warrior surged up, slapping the hooked scythe from his foe's hand. Bolan brought down a hard right into the Haitian's jaw, knocking him unconscious with one shot.

Thinking quickly, Bolan pulled out a cable tie and cinched it over the stump of the Haitian's limb. Bolan couldn't get answers from a man who bled to death.

With that secured, he turned back toward the doorway, emptying his partially spent magazine and feeding the hungry Badger a third box. Once that was done, he pulled a canister off his belt and rolled it toward the stairs he'd come up. A deep breath and swallow equalized the pressure in Bolan's head just in time for the fuse on the flash grenade to burn down.

The sheet of noise and light struck the first man up the stairs hard in the face. The Haitian was at eye level, only a foot away from detonation, and he was instantly blind and deaf. The high pressure of the explosion jarred his brains and sent him tumbling backward into the other Loupes racing up on his heels. It was a tangled jumble of bodies that snarled in the stairwell, buying the Executioner the time he needed to reach the rail and vault himself over, landing on the poolside deck below. Again, he bent his knees to cushion the fall, and he further bled off more momentum as he tucked and rolled once.

At the far stairs, it was a scene right out of a slapstick comedy. Haitian gunmen were struggling to separate themselves from each other. One of them saw the big form of the Executioner rise on their level. He let go of his rifle, then pulled a pistol, but Bolan locked the Aimpoint sight on the fast-reacting gunman and triggered a short, precision burst.

Even as bullets whizzed past Bolan's ear, the gunman's ticket was punched to eternity. Dead, he dropped his weapon and became nothing more than heavy, useless weight tying up the men with him.

Bolan charged to the group, twisting weapons free from numbed hands. He disarmed one of his shotguns, then turned the weapon around, ramming its stock into its former owner's head. There was a loud crunch as he went limp. Bolan turned and clubbed a third man into unconsciousness before the blinded stair climber reached out, jabbing his thumb into the warrior's eye with a lucky grope.

The Executioner staggered backward, clutching his burning, hurting orb. It was a natural human reflex, and he had to exert his will to pull his hand back into the fight, reaching for the blind Haitian's wrist. Using all of his strength and leverage, Bolan twisted and hauled the lucky man to the ground, bouncing him face-first off the concrete.

He turned back to see the last conscious Loupe scrambling for a MAC-11. Bolan whipped out a sidekick that caught him right behind the jaw. Bones shattered under the violent impact, and he slumped to the ground as a nerveless sack of meat. Dead or unconscious, he wouldn't be rising anytime soon.

Bolan went up the stairs and found the wisest of the bunch lying still, fighting to keep his entrails inside his belly. The warrior reached into his small first-aid kit, pulling out all the gauze he had and pressing it against the bullet wound. The injured Haitian's eyes were wide with confusion, but Bolan made certain he kept direct pressure on the wound.

"You'll make it," Bolan told him. "Make sure that Kilo and Tonne know that there's something more lethal than them in West Palm tonight."

The wounded man nodded.

Bolan turned toward the slaughterhouse. He had a dying, tortured body within, a victim of whatever madness afflicted the two Chief Dozen commanders.

And there was a prisoner—the brutal fiend who'd torn that person apart while still alive.

Bolan's spirits were low, until he heard a frightened call from a back room. It was a woman's voice.

Maybe he hadn't been too late for Selena Martinique.

ANTHONY NAPPICO LOOKED AT Selena Martinique as she sat across from him in Bolan's safehouse. She was battered, about the only thing keeping the woman's eyes from being wide and bulging with horror was the fact that they were swollen and bruised.

Bolan returned with an ice pack, and Selena put it against

one eye, sighing with relief as the cold within salved the throbbing pain of the bruising.

"What about our other guest?" Nappico asked.

Bolan looked at Nappico, frowning. "He can fend for himself. He's a medical expert."

"But you tore his arm off with a machine gun," Nappico countered.

"You didn't see what he did to the other captive alongside Selena," Bolan told him. "Just relax and keep an eye on her."

Nappico nodded. He sensed that there was something angry and seething beneath Matt Cooper's surface. He'd been calm, unflappable before. But presently he seemed like a different entity, all changed ever since the "turkey doctor" was caught and snatched from the hotel. There had been one lone gunshot after the battle was over, and Selena had told him that it was a victim of the blood-spattered butcher.

What Nappico couldn't have known were the too common, too powerful memories of dear friends of Bolan's who had been kidnapped and rendered into lumps of mewling meat, kept alive through catheters and IVs while divested of everything that gave them an identity. Bolan had pulled the trigger on them to end that bottomless suffering of retaining a brain but losing everything else that the mind usually controlled.

The Challenger was stuffed as it tore away from the hotel, just slipping through the closing noose of police cars and other emergency vehicles arriving at the scene of the second violent, bloody gunfight that day in West Palm Beach.

The city was on edge, frightened by the war that occurred within its environs. The response was quick, within only two minutes of the final shots fired.

Le Loupe Grotte had lost more than a dozen men at the hotel, and one of their hand-picked torture artists was missing, in the hands of the Executioner. That didn't make things any more palatable for law enforcement and citizens. All that they knew of was another violent attack, bullets and explosions spreading more carnage, doing more to fill the morgues with dead bodies.

"I just…" Nappico began, looking toward the room where the prisoner was locked.

"He is one of Kilo's students," Bolan told him. "He took a living person and destroyed everything about them without killing them. Just like your partner."

Nappico froze.

"But I don't want you in there knowing that. I need to know who was being carved up," Bolan said. "I have the control not to kill him. You might not."

Nappico felt queasy.

Bolan turned and took a pair of mugs off the counter, handing one to Selena, one to Nappico. "Drink up."

Nappico took a sniff, then a sip. It was the same coffee that had sharpened him up to a semblance of sobriety on the ride to West Palm. He frowned, then chugged it down.

Selena was a little more reluctant, but once Nappico showed that he was all right with the drink, she sipped at it. She still managed a shudder.

"What did you do wrong?" Bolan asked her, softly and gently. "What got Ian so mad at you?"

She blinked, as if she were waking from a dream. "I talked to her. I talked to Montoya."

"About the bolt-hole."

Selena nodded, numb. "Ian wanted the cops to come. He didn't mind putting hands on me. Or anyone else. He was crazy, that man."

"But you talked about the hole," Bolan said.

"And the mail. The packages," Selena added.

Bolan frowned.

"This was just before they left my house. They were having these boxes delivered to my home," Selena said. "I just thought it might have been more drugs or something. But it wasn't."

"How big were the boxes?" Bolan asked.

"The size of those copier paper boxes," she answered. "And they were tightly packed with all kinds of components. And then there were the tubes."

"You didn't look inside," Bolan continued.

She nodded.

"Tubes?" Nappico asked. "Could those have been the rocket launchers?"

Bolan nodded. "They were assembling all of this at your place?"

"No. Then the garbage trucks would be by," Selena said. "I didn't touch anything, but the trash men just picked them up and tossed them into their trucks. It sounded like they were crushing it."

"Montoya must have looked into who owned those trucks," Nappico said as he got up and grabbed himself another cup of coffee. He then went back to his table where he kept his USP in its paddle holster. He slid it into his waistband. "Which company?"

Selena said the name.

"That's a big enough company," Nappico said. "It serves both Miami and West Palm Beach."

Bolan nodded, chewing all of this over. "That's how they could transport it. But delivery to your home?"

Selena nodded.

"And no one wondered why you were receiving all of these boxes?" Bolan asked.

"No one cared. Ian had the whole neighborhood cowed. Or all of the cops paid off." Selena took another sip. "But Montoya wouldn't give up. And it got her killed."

The woman wiped a tear from her cheek, sniffing to keep her lip dry.

"We're going to look at the garbage truck lots?" Nappico asked.

Bolan looked at the broken cop. "You feel ready to do something?"

Nappico nodded. "I feel like hell. But I'm fit enough to share that hell."

Bolan sighed. "We can't go rushing out just yet."

"Why not?" Nappico asked.

"I have to have someone take care of Selena here," Bolan said. "And I have to make sure you really are ready to do something."

"I can shoot," Nappico growled.

Bolan remained motionless.

"Damn it, I killed my partner by handing her to them," Nappico groaned. "What the hell do you want me to do?"

"Obey orders," Bolan stated. "And prove to me that you can take care of yourself."

Nappico thought that he was fast, swinging his fist around in a punch that should have laid the big man on the floor. Instead, his wrist struck Bolan's forearm, which felt as hard as an iron bar. Nappico pumped his other fist out in a quick jab, but that got slapped aside with equal ease.

"You're moving in slow motion," Bolan told him. "If you shoot like you punch, then you'll be dead before you can even reach the trigger. Rest. Get your strength back. Get sober."

"I thought I was," Nappico returned.

"Not enough," Bolan told him. "I wasn't even trying."

Nappico's shoulders slumped. "Damn it."

Bolan rested a hand on his shoulder. "I don't need another shooter with me. Not right now. I do need you to take care of Selena while she's here, and to keep an eye on our prisoner."

"And what will you be doing until then?" Nappico asked.

"Taking care of business in my own way," Bolan answered.

With that, he turned and went into the room where the butcher lay, cuffed to a cot.

He was awake, ready to greet the warrior, his dark features cast in an unnerving calm, eyes lit from within by a sullen madness. "Give me my hand back."

"Sorry. I left it behind at the hotel," Bolan answered. This was a lie. Something had inspired the warrior to bring the severed appendage along. He knew that its former owner would have a need to be reunited with it.

"Shame," the butcher said.

"Do you have a name?" Bolan asked.

The grim torture artist remained tight-lipped.

"I'm Matt Cooper, and you're not going to leave here alive," Bolan added. "This is the end of you."

"That's not the way to get information out of me," the Haitian said. "I would think that you'd try to butter me up first."

"I don't have the time," Bolan answered. "Right now, your bosses, Kilo and Tonne, are going crazy all over West Palm."

The one-handed butcher shrugged. "If I'm dead, I don't have to worry about the consequences of that."

"Yes. You do," Bolan returned.

With that, he took a roll of duct tape, covering the man's eyes as securely as he could. Bolan then took a pair of headphones and set them over the Haitian's ears.

"Torture," the butcher said.

"You and I both know better," Bolan said to him. "What you did back there, that's a hideous affront to the sanctity of the human body. This is just white noise and sight deprivation. Stressful. Confusing. Even maddening. But it will soften your resolve to stay quiet."

"Do your worst, weakling. We'll see who is the better man at this," the butcher said.

"Better?" Bolan asked. "I want no part in competition with the inhumanity you've heaped upon people. You win that battle every minute you breathe. You're proud of the horrors you've wrought on others. I regret having to do what I do, but madmen, murderers and worse, like you, they push me toward having to do something to stop you."

"Rationalizing. Wrapping yourself in a cause," the Haitian mocked.

Bolan turned on the white noise generator, then closed the door firmly behind him.

Nappico was waiting. "Sensory deprivation. That's CIA shit."

"Sensory overload, actually," Bolan answered. "And it's nothing nice. It's also nothing our own troops haven't been subjected to in training. It disrupts your concentration. It leaves you off balance. But in the end, your ears won't even be ringing as much as listening to rock music at full volume."

"How long do I leave him in there?" Nappico asked.

"Give it an hour. He'll feel like it was a day. Then take off the phones, not his blindfold. Let him eat and drink," Bolan explained. "And check his stump for infection."

"You said he wasn't going to leave here alive," the cop stated.

"I'm not going to kill an unarmed man," Bolan returned. "He'll get jail. And he'll get what he deserves there, perhaps. Unlike him, I don't abuse the helpless."

Nappico looked at the door. "I don't know if he'd agree to that."

Bolan shrugged. "There will be someone by shortly to take Selena to a safer location."

"How will I recognize him?" Nappico asked.

"He'll have the key to the door," Bolan said. "So if it unlocks, don't shoot him. I also have him bringing you something more than just a pistol."

Nappico tilted his head.

"For when you sober up," Bolan explained. "Right now, I'm in investigation mode."

"You call that at the hotel an investigation?" Nappico asked.

Bolan shook his head. "That was good morning for Le Loupe Grotte. One hour for him. Then some rest. No more than fifteen minutes, then another hour. I should be back by then."

Nappico looked at the big man as he stepped out the door.

He then went back to sit across from Selena with a refreshed mug of coffee. "When I woke up this morning, I didn't think I'd end up in the middle of World War Three."

Then he remembered that he hadn't even intended to wake up that morning.

6

The Challenger rumbled to a halt ten miles down Forest Hill Boulevard, south of West Palm Beach, but still up the road from Miami. This was the lot where Togor Waste Management kept their garbage trucks, as well as some offices and storage to maintain the trucks. Bolan had parked a half mile away, making certain that his approach to this part of the industrial park was unnoticed. He'd pulled in at a sports bar, knowing that he could leave the Challenger parked there for the rest of the night without anyone showing concern for its presence.

In the meantime, Bolan had opted for extreme stealth on this operation. He had left behind the Honey Badger, knowing that if he engaged in a firefight, it might be with honest, hardworking security guards trying to feed their families, and not gun-toting thugs for a Haitian drug cartel. He had the Beretta and Desert Eagle with him, but the Desert Eagle would be his last resort. This was a fact-finding mission.

So far, once more scanning the terrain through his night-vision binoculars, he had picked up the presence of a few men in uniform. They didn't look like they were Haitians, but that would have been too early an assumption, especially at this range. However, the reflection of light on their faces showed them to be of a lighter tone, and their facial features didn't look African.

This complicated things, as Togor Waste Management had little else to link it to any form of organized crime than Selena Martinique's word. Her story hadn't made sense, but that was why the Executioner was burning time investigating. He'd hand off information elsewhere should this be an actual site worth the time of Brognola's growing task force.

But if he stumbled upon Emile Kilo, Ian Tonne or any of the other escaped Chief Dozen members, he'd head back to the Challenger and load up for bear. Or improvise.

He couldn't risk these men escaping. Not with the amount of blood on their hands.

Even so, his instincts didn't feel right about this place.

Tall fences, concertina wire coiled above, plenty of good lighting and armed *white* guards.

Bolan knew that the Mafia used to be big in waste management. Not only was it a lucrative city contract, ensuring plenty of clean, usable seed money from the business and the garbage collector unions, but a landfill or a garbage truck was an indispensable means of disposing of a body. Other gangs had gotten in on this kind of scam, but not to the extent that the old Mafia had.

Early in Bolan's crusade, he'd encountered this scene plenty of times.

Never with Haitian drug gangs. Their business was either strictly drug dealing or armed robbery. Money laundering was most often an afterthought, though Le Loupe Grotte did well enough fencing their ill-gotten gains.

So why send him here?

Bolan pulled out his CPDA and sent off a query to Stony Man Farm. Everything seemed like a diversion here.

It smelled of Mafia, or perhaps Cuban organized crime.

Bolan's questions to the Farm were quick and to the point. Did Le Loupe Grotte have any ties to organized crime? Or did it have rivalries with the locals?

This could have been an instance of Kilo and Tonne cleaning up whoever had bitten them on the ass. Down the road, in Miami, Le Loupe Grotte had gotten big enough to do business with other organizations, but they still kept to themselves, except when it came to warring with other "island boys," which the Haitians still considered the Cubans, no matter how long they had been entrenched.

Bolan recalled the opening salvo of the Chief Dozen as they expanded north from Miami. They had engaged in a brutal, blazing gun battle in the middle of a crowded mall. Their targets were members of a motorcycle gang. The Hoods.

Bolan frowned. The Hoods were associates of the Chicago Syndicate, acting as muscle and support for the long-standing Mafia gang. Simply calling it the Chicago Syndicate was a misnomer. They had started in the Windy City, but they had interests as far-flung as Los Angeles and Florida.

The Chief Dozen had planned to make a move on the Chicago boys, but the Family chose not to bloody its hands down in West Palm Beach. They'd sent in what they had thought were the baddest thugs they could assemble. The trouble was that the Haitians were up to the challenge of the Hoods. Where Le Loupe Grotte owned the southern tip of Florida, as well as large tracts of their home island of Haiti, the Hoods were spread across the nation, even having chapters in Europe.

The outlaw bikers would never have seen themselves having their asses handed to them by Haitians.

Togor's investors were investigated the last time the Justice Department took a close look at the Chicago Syndicate, Kurtzman wrote back. The results weren't good enough for them to make it a part of their prosecution, and so we had leaders squirm free.

The Hoods are still on friendly terms with the Syndicate? Bolan asked. The thing with the big motorcycle clubs was that they developed rivalries with other, similar groups, but still kept their treaties open with different ethnicities. Thus, one of the mottos of the Hoods was Demon Blood Runs—referring to the Demons of Eden, their largest rival, and another international group.

Absolutely. As well as with the Desperadoes motorcycle club, the Engineers, and a few others, Kurtzman replied. Why? What's on your mind?

Did Togor report any of their vehicles stolen in Florida? Bolan pressed.

Running the records...no. Not in Florida, but there were several stolen in Massachusetts, Kurtzman answered. Why?

Bolan didn't respond. He did remember that the Hoods had developed another intense rivalry at the time they were being shellacked by the Haitians. That group was the Wizards motorcycle club, struggling to get its feet under itself and open an arms trade in Florida. Unfortunately, at the time, the Wizards' major arms sources were actually undercover federal agents trying to bring down the club. The leadership suffered greatly, but branches still remained all up and down the East Coast, some groups spread out as far as the Mississippi River.

The Wizards, by their presence in Illinois, had grated against the interests of the Chicago Syndicate, but managed to hang in there.

Did the Chief Dozen have any relations with the Wizards? Bolan asked.

None on the outside, but while they awaited arraignment, they were thrown together at the Glades Correctional Institution, Kurtzman pointed out. That doesn't explain, though, how Kilo and Tonne might have known them.

Martinique, Bolan wrote. She must have been a go-between. Enough so that the Wizards and their stolen garbage trucks were coming to her house, not to pick up boxes of weapons...

But to drop them off. But why should she lie to you? Kurtzman asked.

Bolan grimaced, looking over the Togor compound. Because she wanted the heat turned on to the Syndicate and the Hoods, the two gangs who were pushing against her friends.

I'll let Hal's man know about that when he picks her up. So you're on a wild-goose chase? Kurtzman inquired.

I don't think so. There might be some real gold at the bottom of Togor's garbage. Maybe they just wanted someone to loosen up the surface so digging would be easier, Bolan explained.

You're going in, and you're going to wait for the Chief Dozen to come at them, Kurtzman translated.

You read me loud and clear, Bolan complimented him. Let Hal know that when his task Force is done combing through the hotel, they should amble on over to Togor. No rush, though. I don't think anything will happen until dawn or so.

Which is in an hour and a half, your time, Kurtzman replied.

Bolan checked his chronometer, its tritium hands showing the time. He'd been away from his personal safehouse for twenty minutes. He did the math and figured that he had another twenty or so minutes of wiggle room before he got back to Nappico.

Striker out, Bolan texted.

He then got on the cell to the disgraced cop.

"Cooper?" Nappico asked.

"I might be a little late. Things aren't going to happen here until dawn or so. Give me a half hour past sunrise. If I'm not back by then, get out of there. Leave our death doctor in place," Bolan commanded.

Nappico cleared his throat. "Where are you going to be at dawn?"

Bolan looked out at the garbage truck lot. Turning away, he noticed that there were two more of the beastly vehicles coming up the road, wearing their Togor logos proudly. Things looked as if they were going to happen earlier than expected. Of course, it made sense. The staff of the waste management facility would be getting their equipment ready and day routines into gear before dawn, so they could be on the scene at sunrise.

"I'll be between a rock and a hard place."

He hung up on Nappico, then reached for the select-fire Beretta 93-R in his shoulder holster. There was no time to get back to the Challenger and upgrade to a rifle or a PDW submachine gun.

All he had were his pistols and his wits.

It would have to be enough.

Seamus was glad that the long drive was almost over. He'd been spending the past few weeks running up and down the coast, ferrying equipment to the black woman's home, then picking up other materials. He had to admit the Haitians had a good idea, and was surprised that his fellow Wizards hadn't worked alongside them before.

But soon, he'd be done with the damned garbage truck. He wouldn't have to look at the taillights of the fat, grunting rig ahead of him. He'd have the wind in his face. He was almost tempted to let his hair grow back so he could feel it, but even in his thirties, genetics hadn't been kind to Seamus's hairline. He'd just have to make do with the road beneath him, the sled between his legs and the rush of the breeze.

Before that, he was going to enjoy driving this tank into enemy territory then opening up with the hot little submachine gun sitting on the seat next to him. There were half a dozen men in the back of his garbage truck, all armed to the teeth, with guns even bigger and better than the one in the cab with him. Seamus didn't mind—he was stuck in a small space, and his job was to stay close to his vehicle, if he even had to leave it. The stubby little weapon was the best he could maneuver in such tight quarters.

Even so, the AK pistol, rendered full-auto by the Wizards' gunsmiths, was hardly weak. All he had to do was to lean on the trigger and fire. The thing kicked like a mule, but it would spit out 7.62 mm bullets so fast, the 30-round magazine would be gone inside of two seconds. Seamus had rocked one of these back in the sandbox, not as a full-fledged soldier, but a cook in the Green Zone. That was how he'd been kicked out of the Army, "accidentally" blowing his supervisor's laptop into Swiss cheese with a long, sputtering burst.

But here in the Wizards, Seamus had his taste of real action. He was a powerful, scary motherfucker working alongside a force of nature. He didn't even mind working with the Haitians. They didn't try to pretend to be Americans.

Something moved along the roadside ahead, making long

strides. It was momentarily illuminated by the taillights of the truck ahead of him, which was all the warning Seamus would get before the shadowy mass jumped up onto the running board of the garbage truck's cab. He'd had the window open, and that was the vector through which a rocketing fist darted, taking Seamus on the jaw hard enough to make his eyes cross.

Even as he toppled toward the passenger seat, strong, calloused fingers grabbed a handful of the folds at the back of his neck. That stopped his fall, but wrenched him closer to the window frame. He jolted to a halt when he struck the edge of the door where it met with the windshield. Stars shot up behind his eyes, and the next thing he knew, he was tumbling through empty air, coming to a rolling halt on the asphalt.

BOLAN HAD SIMPLY been too quick of a surprise. The ambush through the garbage-truck door was sudden, but the warrior had it planned out, informed by several other instances where he'd needed to borrow an already-moving vehicle. This instance had been simpler, given that the motor was running, and the driver was, as a member of the Wizards motorcycle club, as far from innocent and immune to some roughing up as one could get.

Bolan checked the side mirror, noticing the driver's tumble coming to a halt in the grasses at roadside. His limbs moved, scratching and clawing, but that was the limit of his vitality. As well, the biker had not only left behind the semi-Krinkov submachine pistol on the truck seat, but also his .45-caliber handgun, wedged between the seat and the center column of the cab.

There were magazines available for the AK-pistol, but the handgun, a .45 caliber Glock, only had one stick. Bolan dumped it, checked the witness holes and counted a full thirteen in the box. He felt the ejector, which was, on the latest models, used for a loaded chamber indicator, and that was raised. The Glock 21 was hot, ready to go with fourteen rounds of .45 ACP.

Bolan smirked. If the .44 caliber autoloaders didn't have not only a longer, flatter trajectory and greater energy at fifty yards than the .45 had at the muzzle, he might have gone to the beefy, high-capacity Glock as his power hitter. However, Bolan's Beretta and his hand loads for it made the 9 mm the equal to most conventional .45 ACP ammunition, and there were times when he needed to hit targets at 200 yards while still having to carry concealed. The Automag and its successor the Desert Eagle did the jobs of a fourteen-shot .45 just as easily, and though the 10 mm version had a closer to .44 Magnum muzzle energy and flat-shooting distance capability, Bolan already had several formulas for .44 Magnum and .44 Automag ammunition that operated his heavier autos.

His reverie of could-have-beens was shunted aside. He was in the center of three garbage trucks that were winding toward the Togor Waste Management facility. He'd seen that they were loaded with gunmen, a half dozen per machine, and there were the sounds of rumbling motorcycles in the distance, shielded from the mob- and biker-owned hard-site by the snarl of the big diesels.

The trucks were going to be used as armored personnel carriers. Using his night-vision binoculars, he saw that firing slots had been cut into the sides of the garbage containers, and he'd noticed the muzzles of rifles set in place. The improvised APCs were beasts of burden, forming a core of heavy fire support. They would swoop in, destroy any gates or bars that would hold off the quicker motorcycle cavalry, and run interference. The more agile hogs would zip along, cutting through places the garbage trucks would snarl up in, spreading mayhem and death through the battleground.

It was a cunning plan, one that Bolan had only barely stumbled onto thanks to the reports of thefts of the big vehicles from a Togor facility up in Philadelphia, and the slim thread of connection between the Wizards and Le Loupe Grotte.

The Haitians had called upon the Chief Dozen to lead their war in Florida to spread out and conquer other gangs who hadn't knuckled under before. Kilo and Tonne had earned their pay with a battle plan right out of a master tank battle. Back in his crusade as a vigilante, the Executioner had stunned organized crime with small-unit and commando-style military tactics, enabling him to complete his measure of justice against the kind of society that had brought his family to ruin.

And it would seem that years later, the two Haitian gangsters had decided to up the ante in warfare against entrenched mobsters. Nothing less than an armored assault cavalry could follow up the brutal, bloody rocket-grenade attack at West Palm's courthouse.

If the Chief Dozen wanted to prove that they were still a power capable of holding their own outside of Little Haiti, then this attack was going to be the backbreaking brick hurled through their rivals' window.

There was only one fly in the ointment. The Executioner had slipped into the assault group. He wasn't here to rescue Togor, simply to kill two birds with one stone. He'd let both sides blaze away at each other, and once the mayhem had depleted the two combatant forces, he'd finish off this stage of the conflict. He'd have to be careful. The garbage truck cabs had enough metal to keep their engines and the trash compartments safe from small-arms fire, but neither the windshield nor the door windows would provide much protection.

Bolan would need to keep his head down, or at best, drive aggressively, never providing enough of a target for the Syndicate or the Hood gunners to riddle the driver's seat with lead.

If it came time to go on extra-vehicular activity, then so be it. He'd need to get out of the cab and take on the mass of killers riding in the armored shell behind him.

One more check off to the side of the road. The biker had gotten to his feet. He was haggard, arms hanging limply, knees wobbling, trying to maintain his footing. It was likely he was yelling as loudly as he could, trying to warn his fellow armored core that there was an infiltrator among them.

Bolan couldn't worry about that now. The bikers would be moving in soon, and maybe in their rush to the facility, they wouldn't see him, or hear him over the roar of their machines or their speed and focus on the target.

But the Executioner had relied upon luck and audacity once already this night, and he'd only survived on skill and wits alone. He had to brace himself for the battle, and realize that once he was through the gates, everyone was going to be shooting at him. His protection, for the moment, were panes of glass and the rolled-steel shell of the garbage truck cab.

Not much of a tank, not when he had two others against him, as well as ground troops on the side of the Syndicate and the Hoods. Bolan knew he had to do as always—not rely on equipment as much as his own intelligence and reflexes.

The radio hissed.

"Seamus! Delgarr! Hit the gas. We're almost there!" came the voice of the lead truck.

The last rolling garbage scow broke to the right, spreading out. Bolan took this as a hint to swerve left. As he settled into formation, he saw that the three armored trucks were formed into a flying vee, and had been spread out enough to plow down not only the gate, but the guardhouse at the gate.

That was Seamus's target, apparently. Bolan kept up the pressure on the gas. While the truck wasn't fast, its engine was powerful, and he was building plenty of momentum to go with the enormous mass of the rolling beast. There was a guard within who pulled up an assault rifle, blazing through the glass at the sight of three tanks bearing down on the entrance.

Bolan lowered his head, bullets piercing the windshield and racing over his head. To the windshield's credit, it didn't shatter or blur with a myriad of cracks. The bullets went through, but they plunked harmlessly into the space behind Bolan's seat. The Wizards had done something to the glass to make certain it would rob incoming fire of its energy, while still allowing the driver to see through it.

Maybe it was heavy Lexan, properly scored so that it would break free cleanly on impact, rather than drag the rest of the material with it.

Another round hit, and Bolan realized that it wasn't the bullets penetrating, but cubes popping loose on the inner shield.

This wouldn't last for long. The treated glass was abating even during the first salvo of guard fire. Didn't matter as there was a sudden jolt, broken planks flying up against the glass and deflecting away harmlessly. The crunch of the guardhouse was unmistakable, though Bolan wasn't certain if the sentry stood his ground or had leaped free in time. Either way, the chain-link fence and its rolls of concertina wire were crumpled immediately afterward.

The Wizards and Le Loupe Grotte were inside the Togor facility and, from the look of things, Syndicate and Hoods gunmen were pouring out in response.

The world around the Executioner became loud as two armies went to war in South Florida.

7

Bolan didn't let up on the gas as he steered his hijacked garbage truck toward a knot of rough-looking, tattooed gunmen who had emerged from a trailer-style office. They weren't security guards, not unless your standard rent-a-cop agency uniform consisted of tight T-shirts and SS lightning-bolt tattoos on forearms.

No, these men were hard-eyed and cold-souled, and their hands were filled with submachine guns that whipped toward the Executioner's cab. Whereas the guardhouse was equipped with an assault rifle of some form that knocked pieces of sandwiched Lexan off his armored windshield, the lighter, smaller guns simply plunked and bounced off of the treated glass, leaving little more than a quickly fading smear.

Bolan fired the garbage truck into the side of the trailer at 40 miles an hour, tons of steel driven by a mighty diesel engine crushed flesh, aluminum and wood all at once. Once more he had to compliment the Wizards motorcycle club for having chosen the perfect tank to utterly overwhelm their opposition.

He glanced at the side mirror and saw that the rifles poking out of the side of the trash compartment slits were belching flame, angling this way and that as they looked for targets. The way things were going, Bolan wondered just how much damage the upstarts would cause before the Syndicate and Hoods defenders began to make their mark.

A sudden jolt rocked the cab and Bolan swerved hard. Someone out there had a 40 mm grenade launcher, as he recognized the hollow thump that preceded the knock he'd taken. The round, a High-Explosive Dual Purpose shell, might have been great for clearing a room, but it was meant for close support, lethal only within 5 meters. Against armor, the HEDP would leave a dent.

Sure enough, the windshield was missing an area the size of the Executioner's head, but no shrapnel had penetrated. Bolan brought the garbage truck around and looked for where that powerful round had come from.

The trouble was, it was night and he'd put his night-vision binoculars away so as not to have its abilities washed out by his own headlights and the taillights ahead of him, and he was moving fast.

Thoom!

Another powerful round burst against the side of the garbage truck, and Bolan saw the shooter throw forward the action of his M-203 grenade launcher to reload it. There was no way that the warrior could pull around the garbage truck to run him down, but then, if he took him out in that manner, he'd be giving up a sure thing that would even the odds between himself and the two forces at play here.

Bolan scooped up the AK pistol, tucked the Glock into his web belt, then threw open the driver's door, abandoning the garbage truck to let it roll to a halt. He was leaving the gunmen in the back as sitting ducks, but they weren't his concern. He was there to blunt the efforts of the Chief Dozen, so letting their gunmen and the Wizards shooters take the brunt of revenge was just another part of his plan. He'd let the Syndicate and the Hoods do some of the work while he made certain that the entrenched gangs received their fair share of pain.

The full-auto rifle-caliber pistol had a lot more kick and muzzle-flash than the Honey Badger by virtue that the 7.62 mm ComBloc rounds were meant for sixteen-inch barrels, not the eight-inch tube that was tacked onto this little hammer. As such, when Bolan fired the weapon at the grenadier, he made himself a brilliant target for all the other defenders within the Togor compound. A basketball-size flare illuminated the Executioner as he stitched half a dozen rounds across the chest of an olive-skinned man who was struggling to reload his grenade launcher.

Despite the lack of barrel, the impacts of the AK rounds bowled the man over, crushing ribs and shredding internal organs in a snarling display of devastation. A couple more men, one obviously a Hoods biker, complete with his colors, the other a darker grunt with a shotgun, turned toward him and opened fire on where the blazing sun of firepower had lit up moments before.

The Executioner was too swift and savvy to allow himself to be an easy target. Even as he'd fired on his target, he moved, getting out of the line of fire from gunmen who were reacting just a few moments too slow. Ripping blasts of gunfire lanced the air he'd occupied only a second ago. Bolan whirled, pausing midstep to bring up the pseudo-Krinkov and trigger two more quick, short bursts that nailed either of the two gunners, puncturing torso and head, spilling lifeless corpses into the dirt.

At the garbage truck, a Haitian lurched into view, firing his assault rifle from the hip, sweeping the scene with little regard of where his bullets were going. One round careened perilously close, near enough to pluck at the leg of Bolan's cargo pants, yet not touching skin. At first Bolan figured that the Loupe was acting recklessly, but it turned out that the initial, magazine-draining burst had been spent to get defenders to take cover.

Even as Syndicate and Hoods gunmen started to return fire, the Haitian was back behind heavy rolled steel, bullets sparking impotently against the metal shell. The gangsters and bikers were caught in the open for a moment, thinking that they could overwhelm one overeager gunner. Instead, they had been flushed, and ended up at the receiving end of five more rifles that homed in on their muzzle-flashes. A sheet of violent death swept from the Loupe killers, and even as Bolan reached the dead grenadier, he spotted a half dozen Syndicate and Hoods guns writhe under full-auto bursts of gunfire.

Bolan turned and spotted one of the Haitian hit men, bringing his AK pistol to bear once again, he sawed the gang member from crotch to throat with a sizzling burst. The Loupe gunner vomited gore, tumbling backward in a lifeless heap.

That drew the fire from the surviving gunners, but Bolan had already slipped behind the cover of a parked truck, its massive bulk shielding him from vengeful bullets seeking his flesh. He scooped up the dead man's weapon, an M-4 carbine with an M-203 grenade launcher mounted underneath. It was a standard setup, a rail-equipped short rifle with a 30-round magazine and a full-auto function, coupled with a quick detach under-barrel launcher on the bottom rail.

The dead man, a Cuban by the look of his features and anti-Castro tattoo scrawled across his forearm, had three spare magazines and four more grenades on his assault vest. Bolan pulled it off the corpse so that he wouldn't need to find spots on his own gear to stow the extra ammunition.

It was then that, even over the crack and snap of gunfire, the unmistakable thunder of a dozen motorcycles bellowed, filling the air with an overwhelming dread as a second wave of horror descended upon the Syndicate's little "legitimate business."

The Haitians who had disgorged from Bolan's halted garbage truck gave their wild whoops of support as the cavalry arrived on snarling steel horses. Instead of lances, the bikers had shotguns and machine pistols that spat out spears of flame and lead to hammer against the mob hard-site.

Togor had been targeted, not just for destruction, but for total extermination. Kilo and Tonne weren't just doing this to do damage to West Palm's organized crime scene, but to cripple the corridor between Miami and the beach city, dropping murder unfettered into where these men felt the strongest.

Bolan figured that the prosecution or the men who had brought in the Chief Dozen had gotten much of their hard data on the Haitian criminals from those who would lose out to a powerful new cartel in the area. As such, the Chicago Syndicate's southern branch was marked for damnation. Unfortunately for the Wizards' deadly mounted brigade, the Executioner was fully aware of their impending arrival.

He'd fed another 40 mm charge into the breech as soon as he hung the load-bearing vest over his shoulders. Bolan had used the M-203 launcher so often that he knew the hold he needed by instinct and he triggered the weapon. A six-ounce shell exited the barrel at a little over a thousand feet per second, sailing in an arc to drop its explosive payload in the middle of the charging row of steeds. The sudden stop it took as it struck the fender of one bike tripped the fuse, and it exploded.

The nose of the Wizard's Harley Davidson motorcycle disappeared, smashed into oblivion by an invisible fist. The fuel tank behind the handlebar fork was ruptured by speeding darts of shrapnel that tore through metal and flesh alike. Soaked with spraying gasoline, the bike's rider was suddenly ablaze, not that he felt much as his face had been shredded by even more shrapnel, one big piece punching through an eye socket and piercing deeply into his brain.

The motorcycle's sudden stop, however, meant that the riders behind him suddenly had to swerve or crash. Some did both, and there was a tangle of machines, one rider dead and seven more unseated by the single grenade blast. Bolan wasn't certain if shrapnel had added to any of their injuries, but there was a good chance that bailing or striking another rider and bike would have been more than enough to cause more than a couple of broken bones. A neck or two if the warrior was truly lucky.

That left four gunmen on bike-back, but none of them seemed concerned with their brothers enough to stop and go back for them. It might have been simple self-preservation, or the realization that they could do more to protect the fallen Wizards by harrying the enemy.

A snorting, bellowing beast of steel lurched into Bolan's peripheral vision and he whirled to see that another of the garbage trucks had turned back toward his position. Either the abandoned garbage truck had drawn them, or they had been summoned by the Haitians. Either way, there was a man leaning out the passenger door, firing a handgun at anything that moved. The machine also had two of the Loupe's men, sprawled atop the cab, blazing their AKs toward the niche where the Executioner had holed up.

Bolan turned his M-4 against the onrushing vehicle, sweeping the windshield with a salvo of 5.56 mm tumblers, then letting it climb under recoil so he could rake the gunmen atop. One of the Haitians screamed as he was perforated and hurled off the top of the truck. The windshield had held, protecting the driver and his aide. There was still a rifleman atop the truck, and gunfire continued to hem him in.

The warrior ducked beneath the frame of a parked garbage truck, rolling and crawling as quickly as he could to get out of the rain of lead and fire. Bolan was on the other side of the truck when there was a sudden boom. The Wizards driver had gone to ramming speed, and only the sheer bulk of the other truck had protected Bolan from being crushed. As it was, he wasn't going to stick around for the Loupe armored personnel carrier to either barrel through or swerve around to run him down. At this moment, the only thing that was keeping the soldier alive was his mobility.

Suddenly, a splash of flame erupted against the rear of the garbage truck as it backed up, trying to catch up to the man who'd infiltrated their convoy. For a moment Bolan thought that the Wizards thought that one of their own had gone wild, but in the flare of firelight, he noticed that it was Hoods rockers on the backs of the bikers who'd hurled Molotov cocktails at the vehicle. Screams erupted in the rear of the truck as burning liquid and glass passed through their firing slits, splashing the Loupes inside with molten agony.

The Wizards driver and his man in the cab were aware of the sudden swoop-in.

Suddenly the battle had grown even more complicated as some of the defending bikers had found their sleds and taken to battle. Bolan saw one man on a bike flash close to another, swinging something. A bloody crown of blood splashed off the victim's skull and he toppled off his ride. At the same time,

Cuban gunsels for the Syndicate were doing their best with the weapons they had.

Bolan fed his M-4 and unleashed a full magazine into a group of gunmen on foot before they could scatter and separate. Firing two- and three-round bursts, he devastated the group of shooters with head and heart shots, killing them to the last man. The flaming truck suddenly rushed past, a motorcycle plastered against the grill, parts of it dragged beneath and crushed under the front wheels.

If there was a Hell on Earth, this was the closest to it. Motorcycle riders engaged in the equivalent of dogfights as defending mobster infantry assailed the last remaining armored vehicle. The Wizards unseated by Bolan's M-203 round were up, but had been forced to retreat from their bikes as the battle swarmed to them. Bolan made certain they didn't forget that there were two forces at work against them by emptying another full magazine into the scattering eight-man squad. It was akin to shooting fish in a barrel—ruthless, bloody butcher's work.

A motorcycle was rolling in from the Executioner's blind spot too fast for him to do anything more than allow himself to go loose on impact. He was surprised by the sudden appearance, but this battleground was too hectic and crowded for even his brilliant tactical mind to pin down. The front wheel and one handlebar rammed across Bolan's thigh and hip, but he allowed himself to fold against the rider, letting the bike pick him up. The collision jarred the M-4 from his hands, but it also knocked the biker's hands from the controls.

Two men and a seven-hundred-pound machine hurtled along like a bullet, striking a third and fourth man with far more brutal consequences. Bolan was protected from those impacts by the nose of the bike and the fact that he'd slithered between the handlebars, fingers digging into the face of the biker.

No longer working the throttle, the machine lost power just in time for Bolan to roll away from the rider and the bike. It smashed hard into a clot of men, bowling them over. The ground had come up hard anyways for the Executioner, even as he hit and tumbled to bleed off momentum and deflect the force from crushing his skeleton. As he lay on his back, feeling dazed by his recent motorcycle adventure, his right hand still pushed down to grasp the handle of his mighty Desert Eagle in its thigh holster. He was surrounded, and if he didn't get back on his feet soon, he'd be run over or shot dead. Neither side would recognize a lone man, dressed in commando black, festooned with weaponry. That would make him a target, either as an invader or as a hired mercenary meant to defend this compound.

The safety clicked off with a single stab of his thumb, and that snap sound focused him, giving him the jolt he needed to sit up, scramble to his feet and look for the closest cover.

There was a garage facility off to one side where two gunmen were opening fire with squad automatic weapons. The light machine guns were unmistakable with their long tongues of flame and bulky forms. Their owners were firing from the hip, and they were undeniably huge men with rippling, corded arms. They appeared to be either sunburned from a long life in the Florida sun, or were perhaps Cubans hired by the local Syndicate. Either way, they were among the defenders and making certain that no one was headed into the garage, forming a no-man's land enforced by high-velocity slugs at volume.

The Executioner, however, knew that whatever was inside the garage was going to be the big prize of this battle. It was likely a storehouse for whatever contraband Togor was hiding and transporting on its garbage trucks. He brought up the Desert Eagle and aimed at the closest of the gunners. There was a sixty-foot death zone around the garage, and Bolan was seventy yards distant. He couldn't, wouldn't get closer if he wanted to stay alive. It was a tactical decision intended to keep his fight going. Losing himself to a stuttering burst from an M-249 SAW's line of flesh-shredding, supersonic slugs was no way to curtail the efforts of the Chief Dozen's return to power.

Besides, the Desert Eagle was being put into operation as he originally intended it—as a long-range weapon when no other was available. Bolan sighted on the SAW gunner and triggered the Desert Eagle twice. He'd reloaded the gun with 240-grain semi-jacketed hollowpoints, adjusting its gas block for the heavier round, and dialing the adjustable sights. He could have knocked over a steel ram target at 200 yards with these bruiser bullets, and both slugs struck the heavy gunner in the chest.

The brute with the light machine gun jerked, but stayed standing, protected from the Magnum rounds by the same body armor that had kept him in the fight against the fire of the Chief Dozen's assault crew. Bolan immediately adjusted his aim higher and fired once more, quickly compensating for the failure of two rounds to the chest with one to the head. This time, the machine gunner's head snapped violently, part of it disappearing as a freight train of lead crashed into his face.

Skull burst like a rotten egg, the Togor defender toppled lifelessly to the ground.

Knowing that the enemy was wearing heavy armor, the Executioner kept his aim at head level, triggering the Desert Eagle twice more against the second of the light machine gunners. This one's head disappeared completely under the twin hammers of Magnum bullets.

The garage, finally defenseless, caught the attention of two surviving motorcyclists who raced toward it. Men on foot were racing to protect what had to have been a great stash of valuable drugs or even more weaponry. Either way, Bolan grimaced as he knew he didn't have anything to make the building come tumbling down. He'd lost the grenade launcher yards away, and it had likely been kicked around in the confusion.

He refreshed the Desert Eagle's load and saw that the burning garbage truck had come to a halt. The windshield was gone, finally blown out by defenders' gunfire. There was a good chance that he could get to it, and it might actually be in running condition. Even if he couldn't blow up the garage, he could at least collapse the building in on itself.

That would keep the Loupes from grabbing the gear and running for the hills.

He charged to the truck, pausing only to put a .44 Magnum

slug through the head or chest of a gunman who looked in his direction. Bodies were building up while the gunfire itself was dying down. This war was coming to a halt, and once one side or the other got it together, they'd focus their energy on him. Bolan had been caught in the middle of an enemy camp when they were aware of his presence, so it wouldn't be the most difficult of odds against him, but they would still have a better chance of catching him with a flanking maneuver.

The garbage truck was his target, and he raced up to the cab. Since the back of the truck was still aflame, and smelling of roasting pork and burning hair, the defenders and the attackers must have assumed that it had little value in the battle and was done.

Bolan was willing to ride that edge of danger. Things couldn't get any riskier for him, and the fuel tanks were well shielded from the flames licking off the metal container.

Another Haitian must have gotten the same idea as Bolan, because he was rushing toward the cab, as well. Bolan charged ahead as the gangster reached to pull himself into the driver's seat. The Executioner struck the Loupe mobster square in the small of his back, scissoring him against the frame of the driver's seat and the edge of the door. There was an ugly crunch from the collision, and as Bolan backed away, the Haitian toppled backward, his face split in a straight line that intersected his right eye.

The gangster was dazed, but he still had a gun in his hand. Bolan solved that problem with a powerful chop to the wrist, and ended this mini conflict with an elbow to the jaw. He grabbed the bloody steering wheel, slick with what must have been the contents of his foe's face, and dragged himself into the driver's seat.

The engine was still growling, and all he had to do was to throw the mighty beast into gear. With a tromp of the gas, the blazing truck barreled toward the garage. Bolan didn't swerve for anyone. While he was surrounded by enemies, he was liberated. There were no bystanders, no innocents to bring to harm.

He stuck gunmen as he ramped the big machine up to speed. Those hit at ten miles an hour spiraled, grunting to the ground. Those hit at twenty let out a yell as bones broke on impact. Once he hit thirty miles an hour, there was an ugly splat and crunch accompanied by a cut-off scream.

He'd cut a swath of carnage through the battle, but presently he was flanked by bikers, their pistols blazing. Bullets ricocheted off the cab, but Bolan kept up his charge, slamming into the side of the garage at ramming speed. Prefab steel folded and crumpled under the same material propelled by a diesel engine snorting out its power. The wall folded inward, petals of metal peeling back under the force of the rolling juggernaut.

He stomped the brakes, trusting the blazing back of the truck to keep others from coming inside too quickly.

Bolan got out, transferring to his select-fire Beretta. Large bale packets, wrapped in plastic, were stuffed, alternating with white powder and green foliage. It didn't really matter if the white packages were cocaine or heroin, he was looking at hundreds of millions of dollars in product that was at the core of a blitzkrieg war.

Someone kicked in a door on the other side of the prefab garage, and Bolan brought up the 93-R, triggering a 3-round burst into the figure. The trio of 9 mm bullets struck true, the rounds delivering more than a half ton of energy at once, thanks to Bolan's personal formula for the Parabellum cartridge. Screaming out of the extra-length barrel of his Beretta at more than 1200 feet per second, 127-grain hollowpoints, would connect with the equivalent of 410 foot-pounds of force. Individually, it was the kind of power that police departments around the nation looked for in a fighting cartridge. When hitting en masse, such as fired from a submachine gun or the customized Beretta, it was absolutely devastating.

Bolan reached for his LED flashlight and looked around for some means of getting out of here and narrowing the odds. There were crates broken open, rifles drawn out of their storage and filled with magazines. This must have been the first thing the Syndicate members had done earlier in the day when they'd learned of the Chief Dozen's violent escape.

The mob didn't want the upstarts to hit them at their weakest, so they'd taken their stash of smuggled rifles and put them to use. Bolan picked up another M-4, this one without a grenade launcher. He made up for the weapon's shortcomings by pocketing standard hand grenades from another crate. He still had a few magazines, but loaded up with fresh firepower.

More shadows appeared at the far door. Bolan let them have another fast burst with the Beretta, then rested the barrel of the M-4 on his forearm and cut loose with a half magazine of 5.56 mm tumblers, giving the enemy the illusion that there were two shooters inside the garage. That would give them a moment's pause.

He looked back and saw that the flames on the garbage truck had transferred to the walls.

Bolan kicked over the crate of hand grenades, then took his combat knife to the gas tank beneath the garbage truck. Stinking diesel sloshed onto the floor.

He had set the stage for this building to become a firetrap, the final resting place for illegal weapons and a king's ransom in illicit drugs. The fuel spread.

Next, all the Executioner needed to do was to get out alive.

8

"Kill that motherfucker!" Miguel Borasco shouted. He'd been given the task of protecting the Syndicate's operation in south Florida, the beautiful smuggling hub of guns, money and drugs that were shuffled throughout the nation in the backs of vehicles that no one would dream of searching—the garbage trucks of the Togor Waste Management fleet.

Borasco knew just how much money was stored inside the garage, and he was screwed if he lost even a tenth of the product within. It was bad enough he had to break the seals on the cases of M-4s and SAWs, expending hundreds of rounds of ammunition.

The garbage trucks on the lot received a lot of damage, but those could be recouped. What couldn't be recouped were two tons of heroin, a ton of cocaine and five tons of marijuana. The cost of those would mean that Borasco would be dead, eventually. He didn't want to know what kind of tortures he'd endure before he embraced the oblivion of death. He'd almost rather catch a bullet in the face.

No, he'd rather have a quick, painless end.

Borasco pulled his handgun, a brand-new Fabrique Nationale 5.7 mm pistol, possessing all the power of a chopped M-16 copy, but none of the overbearing muzzle-flash and noise. He had a 20-round in the magazine and one in the pipe, and he could shoot through light sheet metal if necessary. It was a sleek-looking handgun, and he'd used others like it before. The 5.7 wasn't armor-piercing, but his first shots took out windshield glass easily and then hurled lethal lead into the two would-be assassins.

"There's two of the fuckers inside the garage!" one of his lieutenants told him. "Two different guns from different positions."

"We can't get through the hole they knocked in the wall?" Borasco asked.

"Too hot," another said. "We had a couple guys try to get in, but they came back out, burned bad."

"Sons of bitches," Borasco snarled. "Those Haitians hired some good meat to come after us."

"That's the weird part," the second said. "One of the drivers was seen shooting his own group. Of course, he was white and he was shooting up the Loupes…"

"Right now, I'm not too concerned with who these guys are. I just need them dead, and that truck fire put out before our investment goes up in smoke," Borasco said.

"Okay, we're grabbing all of the fire extinguishers we can," the first replied. "Once we're set, we put out the fire and take the garage back."

"Do it," Borasco said. He rechecked the load on his FN 5.7. If he couldn't get things back under control, show the bosses in Chicago that he had been able to limit the hemorrhage of money caused by the Chief Dozen's renewed, rejuvenated existence, then he might as well save one bullet to eat. The 5.7 mm round would easily slice through the roof of his mouth, destroy his brain with its high-velocity passage, and eject any of the rest out the hole burst through the dome of his skull. One pull of the trigger and he wouldn't have to face a life of pain and suffering.

But he wasn't looking for a way out just yet.

"Let's do this!" Borasco shouted. He and a group of his gunmen opened fire, in unison, on the hole torn in the side of the garage by the blazing garbage truck. Borasco put out half of the 20-round magazine, plus the one in the chamber, feeling the pistol recoil as it spat out hypervelocity projectiles in a salvo of aggression. The 5.7's bark was impressive, matching the rattle of the rifles and SMGs wielded by his allies.

Whoever was inside didn't return fire. That was the cue for two other men to come up with fire extinguishers, heavy-duty ones that vomited blasts of white fluffy clouds. It was a wild spray from the two, both of whom kept their bodies safe behind the sheet metal walls to deflect any gunfire from within. Even through the choking white fog, Borasco could see the tongues of flame within smother, wither and die.

There was the chatter of a gun battle on the other side of the building. Borasco reloaded his half-empty pistol and charged to the entrance. "Follow me."

As soon as he was through the hole, his feet splashed in a puddle of diesel fuel leaked all over the floor. He slowed down, knowing that he could lose his footing. Borasco paused to wave to the men behind him, pointing to the slicked floor.

"Lucky we put the truck out when we did," one of the men said. He had formerly been holding an extinguisher, presently replaced by a stubby MP-5K SMG.

Something hit the concrete floor hard, something metal and round, raising a ruckus as it rolled closer to the group. Borasco turned, eyes widening. One of the intruders had just tossed a live grenade onto the floor, and it was underneath the garbage truck. Instinct drove the mobster under the vehicle, his fingers wrapping around the smooth metal shell of the hand grenade. It was one of the minibombs that was part of the stash of firepower kept here in the garage.

With a grimace, he snapped his arm straight, skidding the palm-size explosive away from the truck, toward the far end of the garage.

It went straight toward the heavy bags of marijuana wrapped for storage.

Better it was that than he and his men catching a face full of shrapnel and burning fuel from an erupting truck. The grenade exploded, a muffled thud in the distance, his hearing long since deadened by the night's chatter of guns and screams of death.

He'd averted a little more demise, a lot more damage among his men. It was a worthwhile effort.

That's when more explosions went off. This was toward the opposite end of the building, where the other team was trying to break in. Borasco clawed at the floor, pushing himself out from under the truck. He was greasy with diesel fuel and reeked of the stuff.

One of his guys handed him the pistol he'd dropped when he'd dived for the grenade. His group had split in two, going around either side of the truck. They were about to hit the enemy from two angles, throwing down an irresistible wall of fire.

The only ones who would be dying anymore, he mused, would be the damned Haitians and those psychotic Wizards bikers along with them. In professional cadence, the two teams opened fire, sweeping the shadows for targets. Borasco would have preferred to lead from the front—it was a position where he was most comfortable as a street soldier. He was a doer, not an armchair general. Even so, he pushed hard to stay on the heels of his brothers in arms.

Something pinged as one of his men passed by the open door of the truck cab. Borasco skidded to a halt, recognizing the sound.

"Grenade!" he howled.

There was no way he could stop the detonation of this one so close to his buddies. The cab split open, ripped apart by a pressure wave that tore the door off its hinges, a gush of smoke and wind blowing in a jet right in front of Borasco.

The Cuban was literally spun around, violently hurled to the floor in a jumble of limbs. He tried to shake off his confusion, tried to get his hands and feet underneath him.

Suddenly, another blast shook the great truck, and the fuel-spattered floor ignited, shrapnel sparking on stone. The puddle suddenly became a blaze of liquid light. Borasco remembered a game from his childhood. "The floor is lava!"

Well, this was as close to that truth as he would ever get. He scrambled, retreating from the sudden burst of flames. More sound assaulted his ears. He couldn't separate the sounds. They were indistinct by this point, so he couldn't tell if it was a roaring fire, incessant gunfire or something worse.

The garage shuddered above him. Borasco looked up, eyes wide. It was the roof suddenly giving way. Gunfire. Flames. Grenades. The building was coming down. He rolled away from the burning concrete, arms up over his face to protect his eyes. Something seared his chest and he wondered if it was a bullet, but he noticed that his diesel-soaked clothes had lit up.

"Ahh! Faaaccck!" he sputtered, suddenly slapping at the stinging fires across his chest and stomach.

Something smashed hard across his jaw, and for several long moments Borasco had the dim hope that he wouldn't die by burning alive.

MIGUEL BORASCO'S EYES finally opened. Bolan had rolled the man over onto his stomach to douse the flames. He'd suffered minor burns, nothing that caused tissue damage. The warrior looked back at the garage—it was burning at a good clip.

He'd almost lost the advantage when Borasco saved the garbage truck from one of his first grenades. Fortunately that hand bomb rolled into the marijuana, splitting the tightly packed bales and hurling product everywhere. Unfortunately, the cannabis was the least damaging and the least profitable of the drugs stored within the building. But one thing it did quite well was burn. Fluttered, scattered leaves and stems picked up the fire from the ignited diesel and ferried it toward the other stuff.

Bolan had grabbed the barely armed Borasco and hauled him to freedom and safety. He'd wanted a messenger.

"Wake up," Bolan grumbled menacingly.

The Cuban's eyes fluttered open again. "Who…?"

Bolan clamped his hand over the man's mouth. "Tell your bosses at the Syndicate that the Haitians weren't the only ones here tonight."

Borasco uttered a muffled, "What?"

"I'm here to put down Kilo and Tonne. But you are on my radar now, too," Bolan told him.

With that, he pulled his hand away from the Cuban mobster's mouth. "And who are you?" Borasco asked.

"I'm the man who turned hundreds of millions of dollars into ash, and the man who saved your life," Bolan said. "If you need more answers, you'll have to do the legwork yourself."

"They'll kill me if I go to them with this. Do you know how much…" Borasco muttered. "They're going to kill me for weeks. Months."

"You just have to deliver your message. It doesn't have to be in person. This *is* the twenty-first century," Bolan explained. He pulled out his CPDA. Borasco could make out the little circular lens of the camera in one corner. "Just tell them what happened here."

"What did happen?" Borasco asked. "I know the Island Boys made a move on us here, and they brought some biker friends, but who are you? How many men did you bring?"

Bolan was recording. His face wouldn't appear on this video. But his voice would be unmistakably imposing. "I came alone."

"A-alone," Borasco said. "No one was helping you in the garage? We had you surrounded. Twenty men, still alive, all armed…"

"You're the only one left," Bolan said. "And you're starting to grow less useful."

"The Chief Dozen came after us the same day they were broken out," Borasco said, speaking quickly, looking at the camera finally. He was frightened. "They brought friends, and this one man. Big. Scary. And he outfought twenty-to-one odds."

"More than that at the start of this battle," Bolan added.

"What more do you want said?" Borasco asked.

Bolan tossed him a .44 Magnum cartridge. "Tell them that you're going to take your chances with the Syndicate. I'm not the only man who's outrun them, but I've yet to meet someone who can run faster than sixteen-hundred feet per second."

"I'm not going back to those Chicago guidos," Borasco said,

turning his attention back to the camera Bolan still held. "You bastards put me up to protect your asses, and what do I get? I have no one left. I'm burned, blown up, half-deaf and hurting like hell. You can fuck yourselves!"

"And you…you better get straight," Bolan told him. "If I see you again…"

"I'm dead," Borasco returned.

"Right," Bolan concluded.

Bolan stopped recording. "Got somewhere to send this?"

Borasco rattled off an email. "You can post the link online, I hope."

Bolan nodded. "I can set it up."

"You've run from the Syndicate?"

"I've outrun them. And outfought them."

Borasco's eyes narrowed. "And you're still dropping in on them."

"And killing them," Bolan added.

Borasco swallowed hard.

"You've got a chance. Use it," Bolan said. He handed the Cuban a card. "He'll help you disappear."

"But why?" Borasco asked.

"You fought to save your men. It didn't work, but you did your best," Bolan replied. "That shows something redeeming. But I won't think that forever. Disappear!"

With that, Bolan walked out of his sight, but remained close enough to observe. Borasco made a sign of the cross, looked nervously around, then hit the road. He didn't bother having a second look at the garage, no recovery of anything. Not that Bolan's demolitions left salvage behind.

There would be potheads and junkies missing a lot of fixes, and gang warfare was going to have to be waged without military-style weapons or ammunition.

This was a big chunk taken out of the Chief Dozen and their Le Loupe Grotte minions.

However, none of the escapees were among the dead that Bolan recovered.

There were twelve murderers on the loose, and his top targets were the lethal pair known as Kiloton.

ANTHONY NAPPICO COULDN'T REST. He could have blamed it on all of the coffee, but the truth was that he was concerned about Cooper. The man had sounded as if he were going to war, ending his life in a blaze of glory against the Chief Dozen's army. Then there was the butcher being kept in the other room.

The killer was due for a drink. And Bolan's words rang in Nappico's heart. "I'm not going to abuse an unarmed man."

Nappico had been giving in to his self-destructive urges for days. And yet, for all that nihilism about himself, his initial urge to hit the blindfolded, one-armed man for all the horrors he'd inflicted on helpless innocents died when he saw how pathetic the creature was. He thought of how Montoya had ended up, carved to ribbons, one small sliver at a time, and the only one he held responsible for that was himself.

The door unlocked, but the sound was so sudden that Nappico actually pulled his H&K USP. Then he remembered that Cooper said the new guy would have a key of his own.

"Don't shoot. I'm friendly," the man said.

Man wasn't quite the word for him. He was huge, broad shoulders wide as the door, and he had to stoop to keep from banging his forehead against the top of the jamb. His skin was dark, and his arms hung like cables.

"I don't think I have a gun big enough to deal with you," Nappico replied. "You have the stuff from Cooper?"

"Name's Toro. I'm here to pick up Selena, too, if she's ready," the big brute said. He put down a duffel bag and looked around the safehouse.

"We were letting her sleep it off," Nappico replied. "But Cooper told me to watch her a little more carefully."

"I got the same word from him," Toro agreed. "She gave up

the information about Togor too easy. Like she might not be helping us just because she doesn't like Ian Tonne."

Nappico patted his pocket. "We took her cell phone. Said it was for security's sake."

Even as he said that, he felt an empty space where a flat, electronic square should have been. His eyes widened. "Bitch picked my pocket."

Toro frowned. "She get to see the address here?"

"No. Cooper made sure none of our passengers had open eyes," Nappico said. "I thought he was just being paranoid…"

"But it's not paranoia if they *are* out to get you," Toro concluded. "Open up the bag. Get your stuff."

Nappico reached for the duffel bag, then saw the big man pull out a large, shiny pistol. The Orlando cop had worked with enough fans of SIG-Sauers to vaguely recognize the shape, but this was a stretched-out-looking weapon, as if a SIG had mated with a Colt .45.

Nappico would ask about it later, if he and Toro made it through. He opened the duffel and found some familiar weaponry inside. The top weapon was a Colt AR-15 Sporter carbine, semi-automatic only. Nappico knew the destructive power of the 5.56 mm round it fired, so he didn't feel limited by a lack of full automatic. One shot at a time was how they did it in the Marine Corps, and they handled insurgents throughout Iraq and Afghanistan with aplomb. He pulled out a full magazine and seated it in the well. A tug of the charging handle, and he was ready to fight.

"Need a weapon?" Nappico asked.

"Hand me the Remington," Toro said.

One Remington 870 pump shotgun, with an extended tubular magazine, was present. Nappico handed it over, stock first. "Is it loaded?"

Toro racked the pump. "Chamber was empty, but now it's ready to fight."

Eight rounds of 12-gauge would seem like a lot in most cases, but Nappico remembered the battle at the hotel.

He dug and found a bandoleer of shells. "Just in case."

"We've already followed all the rules of a gunfight. Bring a long-arm. Bring all your friends with long-arms," Toro answered, sliding the looped belt over his head. He plucked one 12-gauge shell off the belt and fed it into the receiver to top off the weapon. "Let's hope the other guys don't follow all of the rules."

Nappico nodded. He slung his rifle, withdrew his H&K USP .40, and went to look in on Selena Martinique. He wasn't going to be stupid about it, though. He kicked open her door, keeping well out of the line of any ambush. They had assumed she was unarmed, but Nappico didn't want to take any chances.

Sure enough, there was a flash and bark as a gun discharged in the darkened room. Nappico felt something hit him, a hot, searing pain across the side of his head. He triggered the USP twice into the darkness, lighting up the room with two powerful blasts. Twin slugs had struck home, even as he fumbled for a light.

Selena coughed up blood, looking like she'd been hit by a car. The combined effect of one thousand foot-pounds of energy landing on her clavicle, even after cutting through her upper biceps, took the fight straight out of her.

Conversely, Nappico was blinking off the effects of only 93 foot-pounds of energy from a cheap little Lorcin .380 auto, striking his forehead at such an angle that it split open the skin. Either way, his legs went rubbery.

"Help," Selena croaked.

Nappico glared at her, realizing that he could only see through one eye. "Help yourself."

He clawed, picked up the Lorcin and the cell phone that had been left on. He killed the power to it, then saw Toro there, helping him walk back into the living room of the safehouse.

"We're fucked. I think she took out my eye," Nappico groaned.

Toro dabbed a cloth over his face, and Nappico could see again.

"Nope. Just blood in your eye," Toro replied.

"Great," Nappico grumbled. His head ached, and his right ear was definitely out of commission. There was a combined whine and howl that made white noise seem palatable. "What about the side of my head?"

Toro remained quiet, but he pressed a compress against the injury. "No skull damage that I can see…"

"You can see a lot?" Nappico asked.

Toro grimaced, answering that question.

"Just a really bad laceration," Toro concluded. "If she'd shot you with a real gun, or had been a little more accurate…"

Nappico suppressed the urge to nod. "Felt real enough."

"No time for feeling sorry for ourselves," Toro returned. "Looks like someone is out there."

"Get on the phone to Cooper," Nappico grunted. "What time is it?"

"It's just a little after dawn," Toro said.

"Lived to see another sunrise," Nappico murmured. "Maybe we can make it to sunset."

9

Emile Kilo frowned as he watched Selena's phone signal cut out, disappearing from the map on his laptop. The same image was on the GPS monitor in the SUV full of gunmen he sent to where his girlfriend had called from. She was a wily, crafty woman, and enjoyed his power almost as much as he did. She had come up with the idea for a rabbit hole when the Feds were making their push against the Chief Dozen.

She had also come up with the idea of having the law verify the power of the recently released death squad by directing them to Togor Waste Management. She'd intended to call the cops once they were done taking care of the prosecutor, giving them golden-spun bullshit about how she'd escaped from a horrible fate.

It was blind luck that she'd managed to grab her phone when Le Loupe Grotte was hit in their hotel "home away from home." Hours after the destruction of Kilo's forces, she had slipped away and called him, telling him about the people who'd taken her.

There were two. Nappico, that fucking turncoat cop who thought nothing of letting his girlfriend be butchered, and a tall, dark stranger who was armed to the teeth. She'd left her phone on because she hadn't seen where they were going. That was all right. Kilo had the means of tracking her phone by GPS.

But suddenly she was no longer transmitting. The mystery man who had plucked her from the Miami hotel must have figured out that she was in communication with Kilo. He sighed, realizing that there was going to be little means of removing that back trail.

"Shouldn't we send someone after that rat's family?" Tonne asked.

Kilo grimaced. "With what? We've got so many people committed to Togor, and we lost a lot when the hotel was hit. We're going to leave ourselves undefended here, or in Miami? Like it or not, we can only do one thing at a time. The breakout took a lot out of our people."

"I wish we could trust these fuckers," Tonne grumbled. He looked toward the door leading off to a row of cells. Kilo and Tonne made certain that the windows had been boarded securely, and with the electricity off to the whole building, there was no lighting for those within. The lack of connection to the power grid didn't have an effect on Kilo and Tonne and their minions. They had small, portable generators to run lamps, laptops, refrigerators and microwaves for day-to-day work, as well as to recharge their cell phones. Ten members of the Chief Dozen were kept in inky blackness, and any sound made within their cells was punished by a blast of ice-cold water from a high-pressure hose. The ten gangsters were kept under lock and key because there was little telling how much these men would give up for the sake of a lighter sentence. Maybe they were trustworthy, and maybe not.

Either way, Kilo and Tonne were going to keep them locked down.

"Ten more pairs of hands would go a long way toward making this operation go more easily," Kilo agreed. "But right now, we're working ourselves thin, and I don't want to hurt what we've got in Miami."

Tonne nodded. "Shouldn't our people have called in by now?"

Kilo's eyes narrowed. "I'll check the police scanner, but we haven't heard anything on the Feds' tac net."

Tonne shook his head. "You heard Selena. This didn't sound right. It was one guy…"

"One guy against a whole crew of gunmen?" Kilo asked.

Tonne breathed deeply. "And you don't find—"

There was a squelch on the radio that cut him off.

"All units, report to Togor Waste Management headquarters on Forest Hill Boulevard. Reports of explosions and fire on scene," the voice on the scanner relayed. "Approach with caution."

Kilo grinned. "Looks like we pulled it off."

Tonne didn't look happy.

"What's wrong?"

"We should have gotten a call," Tonne replied. "We've been waiting for them to let us know."

"Maybe they lost their phone," Kilo returned.

Tonne glared at his partner.

"Come on, we sent an army in there," Kilo chided. "And when they get back, we'll start cleaning up more. Starting with that asshole Nappico's family."

"Then give them a call," Tonne said. "If you're sure they're fine, call *them*. They could have forgotten us."

Kilo hit the speed dial.

The phone rang on the other end.

No answer after five rings.

Seven rings.

Fifteen rings.

Kilo set down the cell phone, sneering at it as if it were a piece of dog shit. "That doesn't mean anything."

"It means that the bastard who hit our people in Miami might have interfered at Togor. And that's a straight line up here to West Palm," Tonne intoned.

"All right. We're screwed," Kilo snapped back. "One scary guy is coming after us. And we lost fifteen bikers, and fifteen more of our gunners."

"We need to cut our losses," Tonne told him. "Scorched earth. Don't bother bringing Selena back."

"Kill her?" Kilo asked. "She's done a lot for us."

"And for that, I'm indebted to her. So let's make her end a

fast one. Rockets and grenades," Tonne begged. "Otherwise, we're dead in the water."

"I'll get in touch with Wayne, the Wizards boss. He can give us some more help," Kilo said.

"Give the order, or I will," Tonne beseeched.

Kilo grimaced. "They're already there by now. Remember? I've been following our team *and* Selena on GPS."

Tonne sighed. "I'll talk to Wayne. He might not like the fact that we lost fifteen of his boys…"

"Who said we lost them?" Kilo asked.

Tonne squeezed the bridge of his nose between thumb and forefinger.

"I just want confirmation," Kilo said. He clapped his friend on the shoulder.

Tonne glanced over his shoulder at Kilo. "All right. We go on the assumption that everyone's all right for now."

"I'm not saying it didn't go easy. I just don't want to go spouting the apocalypse when there—"

"We've got lots of bodies, folks. White. Cuban. Black…" the scanner voice announced. "Send meat wagons, no one's alive."

"Confirm that," came the call from dispatch.

"We're looking at fifty dead. Lots of automatic weapons. Bikers galore, too. We caught one out on the road walking, he has Wizards rockers," the first voice returned. "He said he was tossed out of the truck, and he didn't see a damn thing. But there's Wizards colors and Hoods colors all over the place."

"Black," Kilo repeated.

Tonne frowned.

"We need to call in some more people. Otherwise we're done," Tonne told him. "I'll try to spin this to Wayne. You call our boys and look for more help from the street-level kids."

Kilo looked at the container. "We need to know what those bastards told the prosecution. Let's hope we can get Dr. Death back with Selena."

Tonne paused.

"You forgot about that with all of your 'scorched earth,' didn't you?" Kilo asked.

Tonne sighed. "All right. You have a good point."

Kilo got on the phone to his retrieval team.

NAPPICO STAGGERED to the window, peeking out through the blinds. He made sure not to disturb them, to draw attention.

The sun rising backlit the group—there were five of them. Through the glare, he could see that they were all packing, long weapons that looked fearsome in silhouette. They were looking around while one spoke on a cell phone.

"They know where Selena's phone was," Toro mentioned, nodding toward the room where the wounded woman was whimpering in pain. "But she didn't know exactly where we were. They just have the general block on the street."

"Still going to be dangerous for anyone going outside," Nappico stated. "Those bastards don't give a shit if you're just getting the paper or…"

Nappico looked at lawns and front walkways. There were delivered newspapers in front of almost every house…except for the safehouse. "Oh, hell. I hope these guys aren't that observant."

"Never count on your foe being stupid," Toro replied. "They'll end up making you look worse."

"Cooper's teachings?" Nappico asked.

Toro grimaced. "Experience."

Nappico's head was starting to feel better, and his right ear didn't feel as if it were packed with wet cotton. He had a rifle he was familiar with, and he'd topped off his USP to replace the two .40s that he'd put into Martinique. Toro had looked her over a little more closely, put clot powder and a direct pressure compress on the injury. She wouldn't bleed out, but her arm was a useless, limp rag that Toro had had to tape to the woman's side.

Nappico's own head laceration ached painfully, but he hadn't suffered a concussion. He could tell that much because he'd gotten one twice before. His mind was still sharp, and he didn't have floaters in his vision, little spark headed snakes that swam around even when he closed his eyes.

That meant he'd avoided a traumatic brain injury. That didn't make him feel any better.

"Should we hit them first?" Nappico asked. "We might get lucky."

Toro nodded. "It's cold-blooded, but we finish this fight fast, we don't have to worry about bystanders. Either way, watch your shots. They're going to concentrate on us, so we don't have to be concerned with them hitting a resident, but we have to know where all of our shots are going."

Nappico focused on the front sight, placing it on the chest of the first of the Haitian gunmen. "Don't worry about me. I don't intend to miss with my first shot."

"Me, either," Toro responded. He clicked off the Remington shotgun's safety, aiming at the group. "It's all the rest I'm worried about."

This will get ugly, Nappico thought. He had one solid target, and then the enemy would be moving. The only saving grace would be that they were shooting at Toro and him. The only ones hit would be them—or the torture doctor, or the deceptive Martinique. The house would contain all of their fire.

He thumbed the safety off. "On three…"

That's when a car appeared at the corner. Nappico and Toro held off, realizing that if they started the gunfight just then, an innocent driver would likely be caught in the middle.

The Dodge Challenger snorted as it rolled to a halt.

BOLAN KNEW HE SHOULD TRY to get an hour or so of sleep to restore himself. A little food, a little drink and relaxation for a tiny bit would be all that was necessary to put him back in fighting trim. He had taken a knock or two this night, but nothing that his well-toned physique couldn't absorb. No bullets or blades had penetrated his flesh.

The Challenger turned the corner onto the street where his safehouse waited, and Bolan put on the brakes. There were five men on the road, all of them holding assault rifles. They were black, with the swagger and self-importance of other Haitian gangsters he had seen earlier this night. What cinched it was the idling black SUV parked in the road, and they were looking straight at his safehouse.

This also happened to be a Latino neighborhood, not a Haitian or Jamaican street.

Bolan tapped the gas, letting the big V8 growl to get the Haitians' attention. With that, Bolan opened his car door and stepped out, fully loaded Desert Eagle on a tied-down quick-draw holster. He'd switched his ammunition from the regular 240-grain hollowpoints to the Glaser Safety rounds as he'd headed back to a residential neighborhood. It would have been easy to let such things slide, but the Executioner knew that slacking off on his responsibilities would only make things more dangerous for the people around him.

He'd been called a vigilante early in his War Everlasting, but the truth was that he was a vigilant man, ever watchful, ever mindful of his duty and responsibility. Slacking on any front would lead to his failure, even if that failure was a stray 240-grain hollowpoint punching through a window into a residential home.

He glared at the five men in the street.

"You're in my driveway," he called out to the group.

"And who are you?" the leader of the Haitians asked. He hadn't seen Bolan's quick-draw holster and gun, thanks to the car door. The Beretta was lying on the seat in its shoulder harness.

"None of your damned business," Bolan returned.

All five men immediately became tense, glaring at him. He was antagonizing them, focusing their attention away from the safehouse and dead onto him. If a shooting match were to begin, Bolan had a car door for cover, and the only thing hurt on his side would be some fine, high-speed Detroit steel.

"You ain't know anything about Selena, ain't you?" a second man asked. His words were mushy, and his grammar and vocabulary weren't the best, but what he lost in linguistic skill, however, was more than made up for by token of the brutal-looking AK-74 in his hands. It was aimed at the street, and his finger was off the trigger. He was obviously no virgin when it came to professional firearms handling.

"Selena? You mean, Kilo's girl?" Bolan snapped back. "What about her?"

Then the Chief Dozen hired guns started to spread out. They held their fire, but Bolan was prodding them, keeping them distracted. Out of the corner of one eye he could see that Nappico or someone was in the window of the safehouse, obscured by blinds and window glare from head-on, but at this angle, he could see the human shape.

He also noticed a rifle.

Toro had arrived. The ex-DEA blacksuit must have parked a block over, so as to avoid a situation where his ride would be hemmed in by a vehicle in the middle of the street.

Even as he was monitoring the activities of the gunmen ahead of him, he was weighing the possibilities for making an escape. Bolan would have liked to take Martinique with him to grill her some more, and then work on the silent torturer, but if the Challenger took too many hits, he wouldn't have the transportation for them.

"You talking about our man," the professional gunman said up to Bolan. "He ain't care about her. He just want his doctor back."

"Tell him to suck two bullets and call me in the morning," Bolan returned. His hand was close to the butt of the Desert Eagle. Shoulders loose, feet spread, but balanced, he was in a position to move instantly off the axis of enemy fire as well as to open up on them.

The air was tense. This whole conversation felt as if it were taking an hour, but in reality, this mental chess game was taking less than a minute. Idly, he imagined his smart-ass friend, Hermann Schwarz, giving a whistle from an old spaghetti Western over this showdown.

The only soundtrack that Bolan had, though, were the beats of his heart and the early-morning chirps of waking birds.

"Man, you don't need to die," the pro said, taking a step closer to Bolan. His arms were tense, and he was coiled, ready to shoulder the rifle and fire.

"Maybe you do," Bolan countered.

"Smoke this bitch!" the spokesman snapped.

The pro was about to say something to halt the others, but his fellow Haitians were hauling their hardware up, firing from the hip at the Executioner and his ride.

Bolan crouched low, letting the door take a couple of rounds as he leveled the Desert Eagle at one of the hip-firing goons. The trigger broke cleanly, and a capsule of BB pellets suspended in epoxy and wrapped in copper took off at high velocity, searing across the space between the two of them.

The .44 Magnum slug hit the Haitian, and in an instant, the scored copper jacket broke as it pierced human flesh. But the shell had done its job delivering its contents—300 projectiles vomiting from the flattened flower of metal, producing a destructive cone of hell that macerated human flesh, puncturing lungs and blood vessels. The Chief Dozen gunman took the impact and twisted violently, dropping to the ground as the AK-74 tumbled from lifeless fingers.

At the moment the first gunshots were fired, bullets were whizzing past Bolan's shoulder and plunking into the front of the Challenger, the crash of breaking glass accompanied by the familiar pop of 5.56 mm rounds and 12 gauge booms. Two of the Haitian gun thugs were sideswiped, blasted off their feet by precision fire.

Suddenly the odds were much more even as the Executioner was facing two assassins instead of five, but one of the Haitians whipped toward the safehouse, triggering his rifle. While Bolan cared about the fates of Nappico and Toro, there was the saving grace that they were behind the cover of the front wall, and the Loupe's fire was going to be stopped by the time it reached the back wall of the safehouse. The warrior needed to make certain that this fight was over as fast as possible.

The pro, however, remained focused on Bolan, sidestepping toward the SUV to use it as cover. Even as he moved, he triggered his weapon, not on full-auto, but nearly as fast as his finger worked the trigger, punching out slugs into the door and close enough to Bolan's head to make him drop to the asphalt for cover.

Bolan fired two more Glaser Safety rounds at the Chief Dozen gunman, shooting beneath the car door, but his bullets careened off the asphalt behind where the Haitian gunman's legs and feet should have been. The professional was moving to cover, getting out of the way of Bolan's return fire.

The gunman knew his business, which meant that the Executioner immediately slipped into a higher gear. Haitian gangs were no less dangerous than terrorist groups, but they operated on different tactics. This gunman might have been trained in small arms and small unit combat by the military, which meant that the soldier had to reset himself to a different set of rules. The fact that the gunman got his exposed feet and legs behind the solid cover of tires and wheel axles showed he knew the dynamics of a gunfight.

Once upon a time, this pro had been a soldier on the same side. However, presently he was working for Le Loupe Grotte; he was part of a group who had committed mass murder. He had to be stopped, and Bolan had to put him down without delay.

Bolan broke left, hearing the rifleman shooting at the safehouse let out a death scream as he was slammed by a wall of 12-gauge and 5.56 mm devastation. Toro and Nappico had survived the initial salvo of devastation the Chief Dozen minion had unleashed on the safehouse. They'd returned with the fury of precision gunfire. Chunks of the Haitian sprayed out across the street under the multiple impacts.

That left Bolan one-on-one with a trained rifleman while all he had was his Desert Eagle. He dumped the magazine, pushing home a fresh stick of .44 Magnum Glaser Safety rounds.

The bullets had done their job, destroying themselves against the street instead of continuing along as densely packed lead missiles capable of punching through wood or glass. The trouble was that he was dealing with a smart killer who kept himself to cover.

The Executioner knew better than to fight fair against such a man. If he played the enemy's game, he'd be playing catch-up. With a surge to his feet, he ran toward the SUV that the pro had hidden behind, hurling himself up onto the hood with a powerful leap. The enemy gunman had been expecting a flanking maneuver, but Bolan took the quickest, most direct route, advancing to the roof of the SUV, feeling it buckle under the combined weight of his 200-pound frame and his gear harness. The roof held long enough for Bolan to jump off, spearing feet-first into his opponent's chest.

The Haitian had been primed to turn left or right, but tucked near to the car for protection, he'd ended up right under the soldier. The two-legged kick, backed by two-hundred-fifty pounds of mass and rage, sprawled the assassin onto the concrete.

Even as he fell, Bolan pulled the trigger on his Desert Eagle, punching a 135-grain packet of shot and copper jacketing into the Haitian's face. Skull bone ruptured the copper egg holding hundreds of pellets inside, but that bone had cracked under the collision. Bird-shot exploded through the crease in the Haitian's skull, erupting into the poor bastard's brain pan, shredding gray matter into a soup of brain and bullet. The pro didn't feel a thing as his clavicle broke on the concrete beneath his executioner's weight.

Bolan took a few steps to recover his footing, then looked to the safehouse.

"Striker?" Toro asked.

"Where's your wheels?" Bolan countered.

"Two blocks that way," Toro answered. "Why?"

"I'll give you a lift," Bolan said. "We need to load you up. Martinique is bent…"

"We know," Nappico called out. "Why do you have to drive him to his car?"

"We don't have time to wait around. Take my Challenger and see if it works. I'll confiscate the Haitians' SUV," Bolan told him. "Let's move it. Law enforcement is busy a little farther south, but someone will be coming after all of this shooting. We need to clear out now."

Bolan had to wonder just how much Martinique had compromised the Executioner's operation.

10

Bolan had Selena Martinique's phone hooked up to his CPDA and was in the middle of uploading all of the information within to Stony Man Farm. From there, Aaron Kurtzman and his cyberwizard crew would dig in and find out just what the Haitian gang leader's girlfriend had given up, or had stored in her phone's memory.

Bolan was looking over the phone numbers copied onto the CPDA and bouncing them off Nappico, who might have known a few things about the local players. Unfortunately, Nappico's area of expertise was in Miami, farther south, so he wouldn't be much use for the West Palm Beach IDs. However, Nappico did recognize three numbers from the Miami area.

"That second one is the hotel you smacked last night," Nappico told him. "The other two, they sound familiar…"

"You can't put a finger on it?" Bolan asked.

Nappico glanced toward Bolan, frowning. "I've been doing without sleep and sucking down alcohol. I'm surprised that I have brain cells left."

Bolan nodded. "All right."

"I… Let me take a look at something," Nappico returned. He pulled out his own phone and ran through the list. "Yep, that's what I thought. The first one is one of my CIs."

Bolan took notice of that. That Martinique was calling one of Nappico's confidential informants meant that she very likely had been steering the investigation that Nappico and his partner Montoya had been working on. It was she who had pulled the pair into an untenable situation.

"The other?" Bolan asked.

Nappico shook his head. "I can't place it, but it's on the tip of my tongue."

Bolan rested a hand on the defeated cop's shoulder. "Relax and it will come back to you. We both need a rest."

"Any word on Martinique?" Nappico asked.

"Selena is in surgery now. You put her down good and hard, but she should pull through," Bolan said. "She'll live to make trial. And she'll get the needle."

"I thought you were outside the law," Nappico commented.

"I am. But when I have the opportunity, I make certain that the law has everything it needs to do its job," Bolan explained. "It's a flawed system, but it's still one of the best out there."

Nappico looked at his phone. "I haven't called my family yet."

"They have people looking in on them," Bolan said. "Good men."

Nappico narrowed his eyes. "You vouch for them?"

Bolan nodded.

"Then I'll be good," Nappico returned.

Bolan pushed Nappico into the room where he was bunked. Bolan himself had his own room, but even though his eyelids hung heavily, threatening to snap shut on him, he needed some food. He threw a microwavable pita pocket into the microwave and let it cook for two minutes. In the meantime, he poured himself some milk. The vitamins in the milk would replenish his strength.

Once the pocket was done, he ate it slow. All the while, his mind was going through the facts he had available to him.

The first fact was that there had been no sign of the other members of the Chief Dozen seen aside from Kilo and Tonne. That meant that the two Loupe assassins had either arranged safe passage for them, or they were keeping them locked up. He had notes from the prosecution about the captured group leaders offering information for reduced sentences.

The second fact was that the pair had allied themselves, bolstering their forces with the Wizards motorcycle club. Bolan wasn't certain how much of that allegiance was going to remain after the botched raid on Togor Waste Management.

The third fact was that a lot of firepower had been used, but Kilo and Tonne hadn't had rocket and grenade launchers for the Togor raid. Whether they had used up the high explosives or didn't want to inadvertently lose the Syndicate contraband they had gone after was open to speculation. The Executioner hoped that it was the first case, but he would operate as if Le Loupe Grotte still had RPG-7s and AT-4 rocket launchers in their quiver.

The fourth fact was that Miami was still a stronghold for the Loupes, and Bolan had struck a mighty blow, but nothing fatal. The only thing that seemed to be slowing Kilo and Tonne was that the Haitian drug gang had to keep its day-to-day operations going, all while making their move against the embedded West Palm crime scene. This was an expansion, version 2.0, taking the viciousness of the original assaults and ramping them up.

Even as the warrior chewed on a broccoli, cheese and chicken pocket, he was setting up possibilities for the two Haitian gang lords' future movements. The group sent to retrieve Martinique had been well-armed, but small. Bolan wondered how much of the Loupe forces had fallen under his efforts. Brognola and the task force were still counting and sorting corpses back at Togor.

The Haitians were businessmen, and they were trying to grow their empire. They had declared war on two fronts—one against West Palm and Miami's other organized crime franchises, and another against Florida law enforcement. That meant that they were far from finished. They wouldn't stir up a hornet's nest among both sides of the law without a good reason.

Kilo and Tonne could have remained completely under the radar, hiding their involvement, but they'd dropped off a video of torture revealing that they had survived, and implicating themselves in the murder of a policewoman.

Yet they seemed to be savvy and skilled enough to have

duped Bolan into what could have been a three-way battle with law enforcement involved if Martinique had given her "clues" to actual lawmen and not the Executioner.

Fortunately, instead of what could have been a three-way massacre, Bolan had taken the two involved sides and destroyed them, balancing the odds of each force until they had whittled themselves down so that he could eliminate the winners. But if it had been the police…

All Bolan could think of was that Kiloton was cleaning house against the Chief Dozen.

And if the balance of power shifted in their direction, so much the better.

All the signs pointed to the two gangsters heading into an all-out effort to achieve their goals. The attack on the courthouse was explosive overkill. The battle at Togor actually looked tactically sound, but there were no grenades, no rockets, no heavy artillery that would be a force multiplier to even the odds. Bolan sent out a text to see if there was tension between the Wizards and Le Loupe Grotte.

With that last thought, Bolan lay on his cot, set the alarm on his watch for an hour and a half, and closed his eyes. It wasn't even eight in the morning, but the Executioner doubted that the Haitian killers would make a move this early in the day.

BROGNOLA LOOKED AROUND the wreckage of the waste management company. Flames licked at buildings, holes blown in several. The wreckage of garbage trucks, some torn open by grenades, was strewed around, many of the gutted vehicles revealing a belly full of drugs, counterfeit money and illegally imported military hardware. This was undoubtedly a site where the Executioner had struck. He could even tell where Bolan had been, following the trail of blank-based, unmarked .44 Magnum and 9 mm shell casings that evidence technicians picked up and registered as anomalies in comparison to the other weapons used.

The crime scene techs managed to check most of the ammu-

nition, sifting it into two types—Russian steel-jacketed ammunition that matched the on-site stores that hadn't been burned
up by the fires, and South American-manufactured rounds for
the Chief Dozen's strike force.

"This is a hell of a mess," Buck Greene murmured as he accompanied Brognola. Greene was a good man, and Brognola
hated that such a skilled, talented man was stuck playing nurse-
maid for him. Brognola could take care of himself, but Greene
was the director of security for Stony Man Farm, and opted to
keep an eye on his boys in the field.

"We're definitely going to be playing catch-up with Striker
for a while," Brognola said. "You are positive about the colors
of the two biker groups?"

Greene nodded.

"The Hoods are generally working extra muscle for the Chicago Syndicate," Brognola mused. "And the Wizards have little
love for them."

"The enemy of my enemy is my friend?" Greene asked.

"Looking at the bodies, it doesn't look like this was a friend
operation," Brognola countered. "It was more like we'll use the
other batch of sorry bastards as cannon fodder while we take
care of our business."

"Hell of a prize," Greene added, pointing to the garage.
"Well, what's left of it."

"We have enough of a sample to figure out what they had,"
Brognola returned. "But not enough left to warrant hitting up
the police contraband's warehouse for a robbery."

Greene frowned. "Never said Striker didn't think ahead."

"What else is new?" Brognola asked.

"Toro phoned in. There was a small group sent out to hit
Selena Martinique and another of Striker's prisoners," Greene
replied. "He brought one of them to task force headquarters,
and Martinique is currently in recovery at the hospital. Seems
she tried some business and got two .40s in her upper chest for
her worries."

Brognola grimaced. "But she's alive."

"And Aaron and the team are working on her cell phone. Striker already texted that one of the numbers was to an informant kept by Nappico," Greene said.

"This is getting stickier and nastier," Brognola returned. "What about the prisoner?"

"He's been softened up by white noise and lack of sleep," Greene answered. "The task force has some good interrogators on his case, once the doctors okay him."

"What happened? Did he try something, too?" Brognola inquired.

Greene shook his head. "Arm was blown off on full-auto. Striker tourniquetted the stump, and performed some more first aid."

Brognola frowned. "All right. Are we sure the doctors will okay his interrogation?"

Greene nodded. "He's in great health. Plus, the medics know the interrogators. We're not pulling any torture or water boarding."

"So they're open for anything," Brognola replied. "Anything that we'd normally do."

Greene smiled. "Good to be working with professionals."

"Where else do we get people for the blacksuit program?" Brognola asked. "The country is full of good, honest operators and lawmen. Otherwise, we couldn't run Stony Man so well."

"I know this," Greene responded. "I'm just surprised at the lack of egos we're encountering this time out."

"They lost their own, and they want justice," Brognola said. "And we're going to help them get that."

Greene checked his phone. "Got word from our boys Johnson and Johnson."

Brognola couldn't conceal a smirk. "What's with them?"

"They're sitting on Zoe Sifuentes' place, and things are real quiet," Greene stated.

Brognola tilted his head. "How is that news?"

"It's news because that means whatever Striker did last night, he seriously put a dent in Le Loupes," Greene responded. "Those two have been phoning around to get more info on 'island boy' activity from friends in West Palm and Miami, but things are locked down, and even the stoop sellers are paranoid as cockroaches."

Brognola nodded. "That is good news. We don't have to worry about the Haitians making any more big hits."

"So far," Greene mused.

"You've got something gnawing at your gut?" Brognola asked.

Greene grimaced. "This seems to be going a little too easy. I mean, look around. Do you think that three garbage trucks and two dozen men could have done much to a hard-site like this?"

"This was a trap," Brognola murmured.

"They came in, balls to the wall, but they came in two separate groups. How the hell are the Haitians supposed to know who are their guys and who are Hoods?" Greene explained.

"It'd be chaos, except that there were two Wizards drivers," Brognola stated.

"That doesn't mean the gun ports are going to be any more illuminated," Greene countered. "Shit just doesn't feel good to me. There's murmurs among the rest of the investigators. This was a suicide mission. The Haitians and bikers were facing three-to-one odds."

"Where's the third Wizards driver?" Brognola asked.

"Florida State Police picked him up trying to flag a ride back to West Palm," Greene said. "The only survivor, and that's just because Striker didn't waste a bullet on him."

"We getting anything from him?" Brognola asked.

Greene made a disgusted face. "He's tight-lipped."

"So much for that," Brognola mused. "Put someone from the Farm on him."

"I'll get to it," Greene replied.

Brognola frowned as the security chief turned to his phone. In the meantime, the head Fed thought about the instincts of the task force investigators. The Haitians had come with machine pistols and rifles against a defending force armed with grenade launchers and light machine guns. They were sent to their deaths, but in such a manner that their demise would have been loud, ugly and bloody for both sides.

He fired up the line to Kurtzman.

"What do you need, boss?" came the man's voice over his phone.

"Did Striker ask anything about the Wizards and the Loupes?" Brognola asked.

There was a pause, a moment of stunned silence that Brognola could feel. "Yeah. He's been thinking overtime on this. Asked me to see if there was any friction between the two groups."

"What did you get?" Brognola asked.

"Normally the Wizards got on fine with the Chief Dozen who had been captured alive," Kurtzman explained. "But Kilo and Tonne didn't want to deal with them because their last Florida chapter had been hit hard by ATF undercover cops."

"They were damaged goods," Brognola said. "How did that turn out?"

"There were informants inside the Wizards who helped develop leads to the Chief Dozen," Kurtzman continued. "The prosecutors kept the names out of discovery, and worked backward from the information presented to build up some solid leads, but something must have slipped out."

"And so we have fourteen dead bikers," Brognola mused. "And twelve dead Haitians. You monitoring the IDs of those we... Of course, you are."

"Checking to see if there was any trace of them talking to the district attorney," Kurtzman said. "This might take an hour or two."

Brognola looked around at the carnage. "I don't think anything big is going to happen anytime soon."

"That doesn't mean I'm not going to be hammering this as fast as possible," Kurtzman replied.

Brognola smiled. As if there was ever any doubt that the cyberwizards of Stony Man Farm would slack off.

NAPPICO COULDN'T HAVE BEEN asleep more than half an hour when he sat up. The dreams were coming too hard and too fast since he'd sobered up. He couldn't pass out and let his body flop in unconsciousness, as horrifying images blunted against a blackened blur of an incoherent mind.

He couldn't believe that Dominic was on Martinique's telephone. Dom was the one who had drawn Montoya and him to the woman and her relationship with Ian Tonne. Dom had given them all manner of information, all the things necessary for an investigation to creep closer and closer to the woman and her orbit in the world of Le Loupe Grotte.

Dominic had put them in this position, taken him and his partner so close that Montoya had given herself up to protect both of their families.

Nappico felt a cold, ugly rage twist inside him. He was tempted to go this second and grab that lying bastard and ask him just how much he knew, how deeply he was involved in Montoya being murdered.

Then again, Nappico knew that he wasn't in physical shape to deal with Dominic if he was settled in with a group of Tonne's gunmen.

He grit his teeth, concentrating on the pain that built up from the tension of his jaw, hoping it would slice through his thoughts, his self-loathing, his need to go out and beat the living hell out of that turncoat informant.

But there was no pain on earth behind which he could hide himself. Nappico knew that there was only one way to stop his torment. But if he did that, where would that leave Cooper?

Having to dispose of another corpse.

Besides, Nappico hadn't earned the peace of the grave yet. He had miles to go before he felt worthy of dying.

Out of desperation, he pulled a bottle of sleeping pills from of his jacket pocket. He swallowed two of them dry, then closed his eyes. Out of instinct, he turned on the radio to the sound of screeching static between stations. He couldn't make out what was being said, sung or rapped, so he couldn't form something that would keep him from sleeping. It was white noise that dissolved into the crash of surf on a beach.

Within moments his body relaxed and his mind wandered into the disjointed noise.

"Tony."

It had to have been a dream. It sounded just like Elizabeta Montoya. He was sitting up, and the radio static had dissipated into a minor drone.

"Tony."

"Liz?"

The broken cop stood. The room didn't feel right. It didn't look right. Was this really a dream?

Words, crystal-clear and in his dead partner's voice, were rising from the static. He remembered one night on stakeout, watching one of those crazy ghost shows about how the spirits of the dead could use the sound of white noise to power their speech to the land of the living. Nappico'd wanted to call bullshit on that—it was just more garbage spewed out by basic cable to get ratings, but Montoya had kept him from touching the remote.

"You know, I might have to talk to you if I die first," she had told him then.

Nappico blew that off.

The static spoke once more. "Told you." It repeated it twice, three times, five times.

"All right!" Nappico answered. "You're real. You're Liz."

"Yes."

Nappico was dreaming. But was this really a fantasy, or was his semiconscious state the only reason he could pick out her voice, his subconscious senses far more acute than his waking mind?

Whichever the case, Nappico tried to bring himself around.

"Stay."

This time Liz's voice was sad. Lonely. Longing for him. Her ghost was attached to him. He was haunted, literally, by her passing, by his guilt. Fantasy or truth, his mind was working overtime. Was he just rationalizing his guilt? Or was there something in Liz's words?

"Wish you had something more for me, Elizabeta. I wish you could point us to Kilo and Tonne."

There was silence. If there was anything in the white noise, Nappico was looking for it. A sign that maybe he was forgiven. That maybe he wasn't worthless. All he got was silence.

"Go home," he finally heard.

Nappico's eyes opened. He wondered if Bolan would think him insane if he related this story.

He decided that his life couldn't be more fucked up if he said something.

BOLAN LISTENED TO THE MIAMI COP with interest as he related his dream, remaining silent, but chewing over the implications of the nightmare. Nappico, in the meantime, started getting more and more nervous as he spoke, his voice getting higher as he doubted his sanity.

"Don't beat yourself up any more," Bolan said.

Nappico let his head lower.

"I'm a strong believer in psychology and the power of the subconscious mind," Bolan added. "The reality and metaphysics of whether it was Montoya talking to you or it was your brain sifting the knowledge you had at hand, that's irrelevant. You were being told the truth."

Nappico looked up, puzzled by Bolan's understanding.

"So we head to my home?" Nappico asked.

"We have to determine what home Montoya was referring to. Was there a particular precinct you worked out of that felt more like home than where you slept at night?" Bolan asked. "Or was there something unsavory in the neighborhood your family resided?"

"We're cops. We don't buy homes in rotten areas," Nappico said. "So, we're going to look at our precinct."

"Miami," Bolan mused.

Nappico nodded. He frowned as he went through his memories. "For about five years, we were at one station house, but that was closed down and we were moved down the block."

"Why?" Bolan asked.

"Old construction. It was full of asbestos," Nappico replied. "Trouble is, the city had the funds to get us some new digs, but they didn't have anything to safely demolish the old station."

"Because of the asbestos," Bolan returned.

Nappico nodded. "We called that the Old Home. Passed by and waved to it, boarded windows and all. Nobody ever came close to it. All those nice white walls, and not a smear of graffiti."

"Do they touch any other stations?" Bolan asked.

Nappico thought about it a second. "Well, we are just down the street, you would think that would be a challenge for taggers. But no one has risked it. And we've had our buildings hit with a tag or three over the years. Even the new station caught some paint."

"Someone is scared of the Old Home," Bolan mused. "And it's not fear of asbestos or cops holding them off."

"That'd take a lot of balls if there was something down there," Nappico said. "Why?"

"It'd be the last place that the police would look," Bolan returned. "But what do they have going on down there? And wouldn't it be noticeable from the street?"

"No, but…" Nappico's eyes lit up with recognition. "The Miami River."

"The old station abutted the river?"

"It used to be on the river side of North River Drive," Nappico returned. "But we moved a little more inland. We were far enough inland that we weren't disturbing anything in the touristy part of the lower river."

Bolan nodded. "I remember that there used to be plenty of trouble along the river until 2002. Smuggling, mostly."

Nappico grunted in agreement. "So Kilo and Tonne are looking for a small port? But even so, there's shipping traffic up

and down the river. Tons of dry goods and materials are constantly going out."

"We'll take a look at that later. Right now, we should check
on your informant, Dominic," Bolan told him. "Saddle up. We're
going in hard."

Nappico looked at him. "You're trusting me?"

"You were vital in putting down three killers only a few
hours ago," Bolan said. "Now that you've got some rest, and
you can think a little more clearly—"

"Despite taking to ghosts," Nappico interjected.

Bolan shrugged. "I've got my own share of ghosts visiting
me in my dreams."

With that, the Executioner rose and headed out to the battered Challenger.

11

Dominic was in West Palm Beach, knowing better than to hang around in Miami where bodies were piling up. They knew him better back home, especially since he was the snitch for a couple of drug cops. Holed up in a fleabag hotel with the shades drawn, he was stuck in the throes of rampant paranoia.

He kept his pistol, a Hi-Point .45, the biggest caliber and the heaviest cannon he could lay his hands on, at the ready. It hung in his pocket like an anchor, but he could have it out and blow half-inch holes in anyone stupid enough to step up to him. Dominic wasn't stupid. Either the officers would want to know why the cops he informed for ended up dead or dying, or Le Loupes Grotte would decide that he might be too much of a liability for them.

Both ways, he knew that he was going to end up in a hurt locker, and he had to fight his way out. The Hi-Point had two spare magazines, but he wasn't sure he could reload the bulky cannon that quickly. All he could hope for was to get a few shots off and take down the bastards before they got him.

There was the rumble of a powerful engine outside, and Dominic tugged aside the blinds, just enough to get a crack big enough to see through. There was a black muscle car on the street, its door chewed up with bullet holes, but it seemed to be rolling along fine.

Dominic froze at the sight. There was a familiar face behind the wheel. Anthony Nappico was leaning out the window, scanning the hotel.

Nappico's face was gaunt and drawn, normally olive features turned grayish-white. His face was covered with grown-in stubble, thickening and blackening his jaw. That combined with the hollow, dark bags beneath his glaring eyes, and Dominic could have sworn that Nappico was risen from the grave. This wasn't a policeman, this was an avenging zombie who had a car that had been hosed with automatic rifle fire, and yet kept rolling.

"Jesus Christ," Dominic muttered, clutching his Hi-Point tight in his fist. "I'm in a fucking horror movie. Zombie cop, coming to kill my ass."

He pressed his back against the door. He wondered if Nappico had gone to the front desk.

No, the Challenger rumbled as it made a circle around the lot, the black death machine rolling slowly as those deep-set, shadowed eyes looked at doorways and windows.

Dominic squeezed his eyes shut, trembling. Of course the bastard didn't need to ask at the front desk. Living dead fuckers like that, they *knew,* he thought frantically.

There was a tap on the glass. Dominic whirled and fired twice, breaking glass in a wild panic. He scrambled, crawling away from the window. He had to make it to the bathroom, and get out through the back. That's why he'd picked a first-floor room, why he'd picked this hotel. He could be out and free within a few moments, scrambling for safety.

He pushed open the rear window in the bathroom, tucked his gun into his waistband, then started up through the opening...

And barreled face-first into a rocketing fist that dumped him back against the bathroom cabinet, breaking the cheap top and corkboard wood. He couldn't tell what had hit him—his eyes were swimming and his brain was a blur of thoughts and terror that suddenly focused when a hand wrapped around his throat.

It was Nappico, a cut on his cheek, glaring at him. "Hello, you little rat."

"It wasn't me! I didn't plan this!" Dominic wailed.

Nappico handed the .45 off to a big man standing with him.

"Plan what? Why you running scared? Why'd you run all the way to West Palm?"

"Honest, Tony. Honest! I was just saying what that bitch told me to say!"

"Or what? You'd get hurt?" Nappico asked, leaning in.

Dominic knew he was in deep shit. The cop's breath stank of coffee, alcohol, cigarettes, all masking a lower base of vomit, blood and rot. This wasn't a living man. This was someone on the fast road to hell, careening out of control and either a walking corpse, or working his way toward eternal darkness.

Nappico glared at Dominic. Color was beginning to show up in his sallow cheeks. Red that seemed to flow down from his bloodshot, raw eyes. "Do I fucking look like I give a damn how much you suffer? Liz was cut to pieces while alive! And I handed her over personally!"

Nappico grabbed the collar of Dominic's shirt, twisting it, lifting the informant. "I murdered my best friend in the world! What makes you think I'm so afraid of Hell that I won't make your death as long and brutal as humanly possible?"

Dominic sputtered, vomit bubbling through his lips. "P-p-please. He's gone crazy, man. Don't let him…"

Bolan shook his head. "You won't get sympathy from me, Dominic. You belong to him."

Tears flushed down Dominic's cheeks.

"Please, Selena said she'd kill me if I didn't give you her house, her relationship to Tonne," Dominic said, snot running and mixing with blood and vomit pouring over his chin. "You have to believe me."

"I believe you," Nappico snarled. "But ask me if I give a shit."

Dominic shook his head. "Don't kill me."

"Give me a good reason not to," Nappico said. "Because I'm not in the mood for caring who dies right now."

Dominic pushed away from the near-dead cop. He racked his forearm across his messy face, clearing away the mass of viscous goo that kept him from breathing clearly. He coughed, hacking up another blot of bile that landed on the carpet.

"There's shit going on in the old precinct house on the river," Dominic said.

Nappico grimaced. "We know that."

Dominic looked up. "No. You don't. There's serious shit. Where do you think Liz died?"

Nappico's features slackened with realization. "What else?"

Dominic coughed some more. Nothing came up, but he spat out the taste of mixed acid and blood from his mouth. "There's no product in the old precinct. It's an observation base."

"Why?" Bolan interjected.

"They're keeping an eye on the Coast Guard and the Miami maritime patrols," Dominic returned. "But that isn't news to you two."

"We could put two and two together," Nappico growled, his ire returning, his color recovering. "But where are Kilo and Tonne? There?"

Dominic's lower lip quivered. "Maybe. They cut me loose once you two were hooked."

"So you ran when they came back to life?" Nappico asked.

Dominic nodded. "They never talked to me directly."

"But think about it. Where else are you going to hide ten men in separate cells?" Bolan asked. "Regular holding and interrogation rooms."

Nappico grimaced. "More than enough room. But how would they get there?"

Dominic gasped, snorting up a tendril of mucus hanging from his nose. "You going to have to look yourself."

Nappico frowned, then hauled off and punched the informant hard, throwing him to the floor with a split cheek. Bolan didn't move, but he was watching closely. The blow wouldn't be followed by another, just days of frustration poured into one snap of violence. Even there, Nappico hadn't felt satisfaction.

There was a rumble and Dominic recognized the sound of a suppressed attempt at controlling nausea. Nappico spat into the toilet bowl, looking queasy.

"I'm sorry, Tony," Dominic whimpered.

Nappico looked at him. "I'm sorry, too, Dom. Leave. Leave Florida."

"For where?" Dominic asked.

"Someplace where we'll never run into each other again," Nappico muttered. He staggered out of the hotel room, walking like the living dead, heading back to the bullet-blasted Challenger.

Dominic looked back to Bolan. "Does he mean he'll kill me?"

"He only has a little killing left in him," Bolan said. "And none of it is meant for you. He just doesn't want a reminder of his betrayal."

Dominic nodded. "My gun?"

"Trust your feet," Bolan added. "Go."

Dominic scrambled, grabbed his money off the counter and left the hotel room.

Already, sirens were wailing in the distance. It was time for the warrior and his ally to be gone after the gunfire.

THE CHALLENGER PEELED OUT of the motel parking lot, Bolan at the wheel, Nappico back in the passenger seat. His coloration had faded from rage, but he hadn't gone green with nausea as he had when he'd first struck Dominic.

"You can sit the rest of this out," Bolan said.

Nappico shook his head. "This doesn't change how I gave someone else to those monsters, then rolled over to die. I'm going to finish this. And them."

"I'm giving you a chance, Tony…"

"Trust me. I'm not going on an end run, Matt," Nappico returned, referring to Bolan by his alias. "But you're not going to tell me that you're not prepared to die."

Bolan frowned, speeding along the road. Nappico had a point. From the moment he fired the first shot against the racketeers who financially destroyed his family, the Executioner knew that he was living on borrowed time, heading toward the only logical conclusion possible in his war against human predators. Bolan had no delusion that his battles would end with him victorious, having scoured the globe of any and all murderers, extortionists, rapists and drug dealers. His body would just be one more, another soldier having fallen in the line of duty. He didn't even expect to have a grave. "All right. But you follow my orders."

"You seem to know what you're doing, so yes," Nappico returned.

Bolan was driving to the location of the third number on Martinique's phone: West Palm Beach. Correlating the intel gathered by Florida law enforcement and by Stony Man's own data mining, they'd discovered that it was a military surplus store owned by Selena Martinique under a dummy corporation.

As a milsurp store, it wouldn't be hard to disguise all manner of equipment coming in and going out at all times of day and night. Standard supplies, too, such as radios and uniforms, gear pouches and backpacks, would be invaluable to the Chief Dozen's gunmen in day-to-day transport and communication.

The Executioner had the Challenger loaded for bear. In addition to the Smith & Wesson M&P 15 rifle and spare H&K P-30 in .40 S&W for Nappico, he had his AR carbine and PDW in .300 Whisper, as well as scavenged gear from his battle at Togor Waste Management.

It was noon, and the sun blazed on the road in front of him as he kept to industrial districts, avoiding residential areas as the Challenger ate up ground. There was no way he was going to get close to civilians and possibly draw them into a crossfire. The only dead would be Bolan and Nappico, or whoever they encountered. He couldn't chance that Martinique had given a description of the Executioner's ride. She *had* called her boyfriend, Tonne.

As such, he had a captured M-249 SAW in the backseat and a Micro-Uzi submachine gun, lent by Toro, tucked against his leg. Nappico had a sawed-off Remington shotgun in his lap, ready for anything as they made their way to Kilo and Tonne's West Palm Beach storehouse. Bolan was on high alert, never stopping for longer than he had to at intersections—but within the limits of traffic laws.

The absolute last thing the Executioner wanted was to get into an incident with law enforcement. He wouldn't engage in a shootout with police, but with the firepower he had on hand, he'd draw fire, and that might injure Nappico. The man was still despondent, still trying to cope with the horrors of the past week.

Whether he'd catch a bullet from his fellow lawmen or from the enemies he raged against in his interrogation of Dominic, Bolan didn't want him to die. He hoped the man still had some self-control.

Bolan slowed the Challenger as he came within range of the military surplus store. Nappico was tensed, ready to go, but he nodded for the Executioner to do his pre-battle planning. Making a reckless assault would only end in a failed mission and two dead operators. Bolan made two orbits around the block, scanning the building for windows and other means of access. The milsurp store was fairly well secured. There was a ten-foot fence topped with wire. The store itself was a converted warehouse, and Bolan could see that there were bars over the windows that were visible over the top of the chain-link fence, which hid the building behind it by having plastic slats interwoven through the links to provide privacy and make climbing the fence a little more difficult.

Kurtzman had sent him a layout of the warehouse, providing Bolan with an inkling of what might be behind the fence. But he wouldn't be able to tell what was behind the walls, or what was between the fence and the shell of the building. There could be guard animals or motion sensors.

Bolan passed the store and drove on until he could find a building from which he could look down on the warehouse. Rather than find a building, he found a construction site with a tower crane on the premises. It should have been a workday, but the site was inactive save for a few security guards and the odd laborers.

The Executioner told Nappico to wait in the car. He retrieved a powerful monocle telescope from his war bag, small enough to fit in his pocket yet give him the ability to see things a mile distant. With a flash of his badge and mention of Brognola's federal task force, he got past the guards and received permission to ascend to the crane to look around.

Bolan was able to count the guards working the perimeter— and these men were better armed than the men in the Miami hotel. They had submachine guns and wore body armor. It made sense. Anyone who would try to rob a milsurp store like this would be loaded for bear, because they were coming for guns and ammunition. Being a Florida firearms seller, it was likely that the milsurp store also was Class III licensed, meaning that the submachine guns were legal for the premises.

That also meant that these were legal imports, which further confounded the Executioner.

Bear, run the store down for me. I don't want to hit an honest dealer, Bolan texted to Stony Man Farm.

How fast you need it? Kurtzman asked.

Bolan frowned. Better yet, let me get some photos for you.

Bolan put the CPDA's camera to the lens of his scope and snapped pictures of the guards. He uploaded them to the Farm. I'm going to do a little more reconnaissance and give you time to do some facial recognition on the men guarding the place, too.

Bolan knew that Kurtzman would put a rush on the data necessary. The Executioner fully believed in every law-abiding citizen's right to own firearms. It was when murderers and psychotics misused those tools that he intervened.

The CPDA vibrated noiselessly to alert the Executioner to the arrival of incoming data.

The guards were confirmed by face recognition to be felons. Kurtzman and the team spent extra minutes going over the pictures by eyeball to verify and solidify that these were bad men, people who had committed acts of violence, usually in the commission of armed robbery and in racial intolerance. Many of the names were also connected to the Wizards motorcycle club, spread out across the Midwest and along the Appalachian valley, where backwoods neo-Nazis mingled with outlaw bikers for money, guns and drugs.

A brutal dozen men, and possibly more within. The one saving grace that Bolan had on his side was the relative seclusion of the store. There were cars in the parking lot, but Bolan was already matching license plates to owners and guards. During his surveillance, a pickup pulled up to the gate, but was turned away. The driver seemed disappointed, but not actually angry.

He was a civilian customer, likely, something the Stony Man cybernetics crew verified with a license plate check. He was probably there because he wanted to go camping, or needed ammunition for a day at the range.

Either way, the driver was refused. He would take his business elsewhere, leaving the Executioner free to make his move against the hard site.

I'll letting Hal know about this development, Kurtzman texted. But he won't move in the troops until you're done.

Pick up the pieces, Bolan agreed. And there will be lots of pieces.

No need to set up a perimeter? Kurtzman asked.

I've already got the closest noncombatants in the area, the crew at a construction site, aware that there is a law-enforcement operation in process, Bolan told him. They'll get their heads down when things blow up.

Godspeed, Kurtzman texted.

With that, the Executioner climbed down the ladder of the crane to rejoin Nappico in the Challenger.

"This kind of manpower on site is just asking for trouble," Carbonas muttered as he smashed out another cigarette in the ashtray. The office stank of ash and coffee and was starting to churn Duncan's stomach—and this was a man who hung with bikers who left their denims and leathers on for months without washing them, if they ever were laundered.

Carbonas had been called in so that Le Loupe Grotte's West Palm expansion team could have some extra manpower. Carbonas wasn't Cuban, he was Mexican, and any chance to stretch the influence of the Mexican cartels into Florida was welcome. The cartel emissary knew that Kilo and Tonne had a good plan in place, simply because they were assembling their own "syndicate" to go face-to-face with Chicago and its allies down in West Palm and Miami.

The trouble was that this brilliant bit of reinforcement, as well as the spreading and maneuvering of manpower and weaponry, was overshadowed by a blatant, brutal assault that would do nothing more than summon all the powers of law and order down upon West Palm Beach to avenge the deaths of civilians and lawmen murdered in the opening salvo.

Duncan wasn't afraid of a fight with the Syndicate, but there was nothing that seemed worth going to war with the federal government over. The Wizards had been infiltrated and crippled a decade back, and were finally back on their feet, becoming a powerful arms trader for street gangs in Florida.

As it was, he didn't mind that Carbonas and his fellow Mexican gun thugs were all packing merchandise from the storehouse. Duncan had been expecting an influx of new products from the assault on Togor before dawn today, but things hadn't turned out the way he'd expected.

Many of his brother Wizards were dead, as well as a large number of the Chief Dozen's street force. The weird thing was that the Syndicate and their local help had also been struck hard, and completely wiped out, except for one man who was now in the custody of the federal task force that came down in the wake of the West Palm massacre.

Duncan hated lugging around the sheer mass of the USAS-12 shotgun. It was fourteen pounds with its curved 10-round magazine, but after the reports of conflict that the two Chief Dozen leaders' men had over the past twenty-four hours, Duncan wouldn't dream of carrying any weaker of a weapon. Ten rounds of full-power 12-gauge buckshot and slugs were serious medicine, capable of carving a swath of death for forty yards, and if that wasn't enough, he could eject the magazine and load in a fresh ten rounds in the space of moments.

Duncan didn't intend to be outgunned, not on this day, not with a force that was neither Syndicate nor law enforcement on the stalk.

Mystery third parties often ended up being far worse than expected. He remembered some brothers out in California who had been part of a takeover of Catalina. The military and police had been held at bay while the hired army of biker thugs held more than 1500 people hostage. Then someone came in with no warning, no communication by the authorities. The law was completely in the dark about who was killing off bikers and arming citizens to fight back.

In the end, none of the hijackers survived or escaped.

Duncan patted himself down, feeling to make certain he had more than enough firepower.

Carbonas looked grim. "I received news from the bosses. We're to load up the trucks and head out to Miami."

Duncan glared at him. "Miami? Why?"

"We don't get to ask that question. Just convoy the hell out of here, full steam," Carbonas told him.

"That's a sack of bullshit. When do we have to get there, at least?"

"Tomorrow morning," Carbonas said. "Something's coming up the river, they said."

Duncan narrowed his eyes. "Up the river?"

Carbonas shrugged. "We've got to get our things there for that."

Duncan snapped his fingers, and the other Wizards jerked to alertness. "Time to pack up! Anything not nailed down or on fire comes with us!"

Suddenly, in the distance, Duncan and Carbonas heard the squeal of tires and the roar of a V8 diesel belting out RPMs in thunderous staccato.

"The fuck is that?" Duncan asked.

Carbonas was on the walkie-talkie. He had his men working this shift to guard the storehouse.

"It's some dude in a shot-up black car," Carbonas announced. "He's pulling donuts at the entrance."

"Donuts?" Duncan asked. "Send out a couple of guys to shoo the idiot off. We can't afford the cops rolling by."

"We're not doing anything wrong," Carbonas muttered. "We watch him. He might be pulling something…"

The two men looked at each other.

"All guards, report in!" Carbonas shouted.

Duncan glared at his brother bikers. "Someone's distracting us! Get on—"

Duncan was cut off as the simultaneous rattle of a half dozen blasts split the air. Sections of fence folded inward, accompanying the shouts of men lashed and lacerated by flying chain link and segments of barbed wire.

Duncan grimaced as he clutched the shotgun in both hands. He'd been ready to fight what he thought would be an army.

But he hadn't taken into account the fact that this mysterious enemy would come calling on the heels of an artillery strike against his barbed-wire-topped fence!

12

Most other soldiers would need far more time to be clever when it came to hitting a fortified arms depot manned by a small army of ill-tempered, bloodthirsty gunmen. Fortunately the Executioner had spent minutes doping out the ranges, the manpower and the defenses he was going up against, and he had two aces in the hole to turn Duncan and Carbonas's full house into a dead man's hand—Anthony Nappico as his sniper overwatch and the privacy fence. Though the slats, as they were interwoven into the chain-link fence, provided plenty of obfuscation for anyone looking from the outside in—fifteen feet, plus barbed wire making it difficult to see over unless someone was willing to spend time at the top of a tower with a high-powered scope—that same privacy also prevented being able to look out.

This would give Bolan an opportunity to sneak up to the fence and leave several little gifts, namely six packets of high explosives set at different points along the fence's structure.

But first, Bolan needed his eyes in the sky.

Nappico had been reluctant at first. "You don't want me on the front lines just yet."

"No. I've read your jacket. You're proficient with the AR-15 platform," Bolan answered. "And I need someone who is a good shot watching my back."

Nappico looked at the .300 Blackout rifle. "Looks like a regular M-16, but you've got it in a different caliber. Some kind of .30 that fits in a regular AR magazine."

"It's the Blackout, based on J. D. Jones's .300 Whisper cartridge," Bolan explained. "It's meant to duplicate the energy and penetration of an AK's 7.62 mm round, but operate with minimal changes in the regular design."

"But it's a little different," Nappico said. "You've got me up about 500 yards from the farthest point of the military surplus warehouse on that crane. AKs aren't known for that kind of range."

"We're using .308 rounds, which have a lot better ballistic coefficient, so their trajectory is flatter. There's less powder in the case, which means it won't go as far as a NATO .30, but it can still do solid work at 500 yards," Bolan answered. "Especially from a match-grade 18-inch barrel like I put on that one."

"You built it?" Nappico asked.

Bolan nodded. "I've done my own armory work since I was in the military."

Nappico narrowed his eyes. "Damn few soldiers are allowed to work on their own weapons."

Bolan didn't answer that. He could tell that the gears were turning inside Nappico's head, trying to figure out who this guy truly was with all the law-enforcement ties, but none of the restrictions. Before the cop could distract himself more, Bolan ordered him to get into position. "If anyone notices me, you raise me on the tac net."

"No firing?" Nappico asked.

Bolan shook his head. "No. That'd let them know that something's going on. I need to set up my distractions first. If this goes right, their attention will be pulled in."

"What is going to draw that much manpower?" Nappico asked.

Bolan only had a smile for an answer.

As soon as the fence packets of explosives detonated, filling the air with broken chain link and unraveled barbed wire, Bolan stopped pulling donuts in front of the military surplus store, throwing the gear into Neutral so that he could rev up the engine. The Executioner's intention was to turn the powerful

Challenger into a missile, tearing not only through the steel-pipe gates, but to launch through the entrance of the store.

The V8 diesel cranked out noise. He had the driver's-side window rolled down, the Honey Badger clenched in his left hand. This wouldn't be a first for the warrior—he'd learned how to shoot off-hand long ago. The rifle-powered machine pistol would kick, but he was prepared for its recoil, as well, and he would have the gun at full tension, stability provided by the sling and his own arm muscles. The weapon was loaded with a Beta-C magazine, two snail drums connected in the middle, providing an AR-platform with one hundred rounds before reloading. The gun weighed a ton with all that ammunition in place, but while he was driving, he wasn't going to be able to reload, and he could rest his forearm on the window sill of the car.

The sudden array of explosions galvanized the guard force, undoubtedly spurred on by panicked orders from the commanders within. Bolan recognized the uniformed "security guards," denim-clad bikers and Hispanics, all of them packing submachine guns and grim visages. This wasn't a legitimate operation, rap sheets pouring into his CPDA providing proof that these were members of the Wizards motorcycle gang and the Mexican cartels who were looking to expand their influence further into Florida. If the white guards weren't part of the Wizards, they were men from the West Coast and farther up the Appalachian valley, SS lightning-bolt tattoos and swastikas giving confirmation that they were violent white supremacists.

Bolan was dead certain of the devils he was engaging with, so he popped the clutch and took off like a rocket. The gates flew apart, torn off their hinges and only producing a few minor cracks in the windshield as they deflected upward and over the roof of the powerful Dodge muscle car. The roar of the engine didn't quite drown out the pop of autofire rippling behind him, but Bolan couldn't be concerned with incoming fire. He clenched his right fist around the steering wheel and tensed in his seat, left arm and gun held within the automobile as it struck the metal frame and safety-glass doors with all the rage and power of 4100 pounds of Detroit steel hurled at them by 470 horsepower.

Sheet steel twisted and launched out of the path of the Challenger, the plastic sheeting contained between two panes of glass keeping it in the form of cubes, not razor-sharp splinters.

Oh, well, that was one failure of the plan, but Bolan's sabotage of the fence wouldn't have produced more than nominal shrapnel, either. What was important was chaos, especially at this early stage of the game as the front bumper struck display stands, shelving and bodies before he could stomp on the brake, spinning the two-ton beast into a 180. Aisles of shelves toppled against each other, falling on themselves and on gunmen like gigantic dominoes.

That bought the Executioner a few moments to stiff-arm the Honey Badger and hose out a storm of .300 Blackout slugs to rip into a trio of guards who were rushing into the store from the shattered front gate. Bolan kept his bursts short, but in quick, rapid succession, ensuring that he could hammer out three to four bullets per target. Even though he had 100 on tap, he wasn't going to waste ammunition on wild, unaimed fire. Precision was the order of the day, and with his opening salvo, he'd taken out all three of his targets, heavy rounds tearing through flesh and bone easily.

Bolan shifted the PDW around, forearm muscles taut under his skin as he aimed at a fourth gunman, this one a well-dressed Hispanic, shouldering an M-16 at the revving automobile. Bolan's burst started impacting the Mexican mobster an inch above his crotch, three more bullets zipping up through the armed thug to stop at the hollow of his throat. The lifeless but stylish corpse toppled backward, crashing atop a fallen shelf, eliciting a cry of pain from a biker who was trapped beneath.

With that, the Executioner hit the gas and accelerated, no longer going for sheer speed, as he needed to maneuver within the store. He peeled out, still, using the front bumper as a weapon to flatten a fifth of the storehouse defenders along the hood. The biker's forehead struck the windshield hard enough to elicit a vomitous flower of blood that obscured Bolan's view of the "road."

Bolan swerved hard, dumping the bloodied Wizard outlaw off the hood, then tapped the windshield washer, jets of fluid loosening the thick gore to be swept out of the way, leaving behind only a smeared pink film that at least allowed him to see where he was going. In that time, Bolan navigated out the driver's window, turning toward a couple more men, a mixed pair of Mexican mafia and uniformed Nazi worshiper. He triggered the machine pistol again, swinging a scythe of hot, supersonic lead across their torsos that hurled them to the painted concrete floor.

Bullets pinged against the sides of the Challenger, the defending force whirling in desperation to take out the black, snarling beast that thrashed among them, breathing fire and hurling its enormous bulk against them. Bolan bounced another off his fender, crashing the Mexican mobster into a glass display case hard enough to flip it over. Even as he zoomed past, he saw that the hit-and-run victim had been carved to ribbons by broken glass and twisted metal.

The roar of Bolan's engine bellowed out its eponymous challenge to any and all to come after him. He wanted the enemy to charge him, to focus all their might and rage against him so that he could keep this battle contained, sewn into a controlled killing box far from innocents.

The windshield suddenly imploded, a violent explosion striking the hood and peeling back metal as the Dodge stopped suddenly—as if it had struck a brick wall. Bolan had strapped himself in to ensure his safety in the incident of a crash, and the safety glass of the windshield did its job, merely pelting and bruising his face rather than slicing it to ribbons as it came apart. Had the man with the grenade launcher fired a moment later or aimed a few inches higher, the Executioner would be dead.

As it was, he was dazed, sitting in the wreckage of what used to be a war machine. Blood flowed from his nose over his lips, but Bolan's vision cleared immediately. He'd gone from the

steering wheel to the seat-belt release even as he realized that
the muscle car was dead in the water.

There was a trio of men rushing the driver's-side door, grim
fury on their faces as they sought to take the stunned Executioner out of the car and pummel him to a greasy pulp. Bolan
surprised them with a withering long burst, raking them with
rainstorm of 125-grain jacketed, boat-tailed hollowpoints. At
this distance, and at their full velocity, the salvo opened up rib
cages and abdominal walls, tearing organs out by their roots
and smashing the killer crew to the ground.

Seat belt no longer restraining him, Bolan popped the driver's-side door and swung himself out. He'd been forced to fire
a long burst, blowing off twenty-five rounds to take down three
men, but at the moment, he wasn't mentally or physically firing
on all cylinders. Even so, he was recovering his balance and
strength quickly, transferring the Honey Badger to his right
shoulder, bracing the high-powered personal defense weapon
with both hands and using the sights to target men who were
racing up on the passenger's side of the vehicle.

Bolan had regained his timing enough to tap out two-round
bursts at the faces of the quartet who had hoped to use the
stopped Challenger as cover. Skulls burst open under double-
sledgehammer impacts, brains exploding out of cavities to rain
in a greasy spray across the floor. The warrior sidestepped,
backing to find some cover for himself when a burly form
slammed against him, heaving Bolan off his feet and knocking the gun away to the extent of its sling.

The Executioner twisted, feeling two arms the thickness of
radial tires wrapped around his waist. He looked down on a torn
T-shirt stretched across a broad, slab-muscled back before the
vision was temporarily knocked from his eyes and his body was
hammered into a fallen shelving unit. Those muscular forearms
had cushioned Bolan's spine against the impact, but the back of
his head was rattled as it glanced against an aluminum shelf,
scalp splitting on contact.

Bolan reacted even without sight, powering a raised-knuckle

fist hard against the melon of a head that was pushed against his chest. The peach-fuzz-covered dome jerked under the power of the punch, and the crushing might of those thick, rippling arms eased off Bolan's torso. The Executioner changed tactics and sliced down with an ax-hand that missed its mark, bouncing off a dense trapezoid muscle instead of chopping into a cluster of nerves.

But it was still enough to give Bolan the freedom to bring up both knees against his foe's chest. Bracing his hands on the fallen shelving, the Executioner shoved hard with both legs, tossing the brawny biker off him. Bolan tried to rise to his feet, but something snagged his left shoulder and brought him crashing back down, head bouncing against another aluminum shelf. He tried to pull himself free, but was stuck, and found that his collar was growing wet with more blood.

Battered, the warrior wasn't about to take chances with a foe who outweighed him by fifty pounds, not with an unknown number of other opponents still alive and on the loose around the warehouse. He ripped the Desert Eagle from its holster and fired two shots into the giant killer's chest—.44 Magnum slugs struck bone and split as they shattered ribs, sending dozens of lesser projectiles churning through lung tissue. Two 240-grain bullets turned into four 120-grain projectiles that whipped through blood vessels and impacted against the man's back ribs, thick shoulder muscle and heavy scapula bones.

The two-shot salvo sent the huge thug to the ground like a rag doll.

Bolan looked around and found that his .300 PDW was snagged on a shelf, pinning his left arm to the unit. With that realization, he spotted more gunmen rising from the wrecked store. Some looked as beat-up as Bolan felt, while others seemed fairly fresh for a continued fight. They had heard the thunder of Bolan's mighty .44, so they didn't show themselves for more than an instant before ducking behind cover.

Bolan regretted that Nappico had very little chance of giving him cover fire through the roof and walls of the warehouse.

That was all right. Bolan had anticipated that the muscle car might end up abandoned on this penetration of enemy fortifications, and had planned accordingly. He reached for a detonator within his battle harness and triggered it.

More charges of RDX explosives went off, peeling the roof off the Challenger, splitting it into quarters and hurling the pieces out like deadly guillotine blades. Those defending thugs who weren't shocked and deafened by the sudden blast, hurled themselves to the ground as two men were decapitated by flying sheets of ragged metal.

Bolan unclipped the sling from around his shoulder and got out of the trap he'd found himself in. He'd recover his weapon later, if he had the opportunity. For the moment he had to fight with what he still had with him, and Bolan had chosen the Desert Eagle and the Beretta for their firepower, both in punch and in volume of fire.

Two gunmen spotted the Executioner on the move and spun to deal with him, but Bolan's reflexes were honed by countless battles. He put a single 240-grain bullet through the bridge of a Mexican rifleman's nose, excavating a tunnel through his skull. He then turned to the other gunner, tapping off a second bone crusher that shattered the breastbone of a shotgun-armed biker, folding him in two.

Bolan knew that he'd given away his position, but it couldn't be helped. If anything, this would once more bring the battle right to him. He'd caught sight of about eight more gunmen left in the battle scene, so he knew that there were still heavy odds against him. He executed a quick change of magazines, even as he ducked around, looking for more cover. Loaded up with eight in the butt and one in the pipe, the warrior had nearly five-and-a-half tons of muzzle energy ready to fly at any enemy. That kind of punch would go a long way to evening the odds.

There was one biker who struggled up a set of steps, and he was packing a USAS-12—a monster of a shotgun with a 10-round detachable magazine and the ability to hammer out 12-gauge blasts at a rate of 300 rounds per minute. The Wizards gun thug was struggling under the weight of the mighty beast of a weapon, and he was snapping orders, shouting to the surviving defenders even as he was looking to get out of range of the mayhem. On his heels was an especially well-groomed Mexican gunman wielding a Desert Eagle of his own, except instead of the matte stainless-steel finish on Bolan's personal weapon, the drug dealer's pistol was a gleaming, mirror-polished gold.

That kind of money for a personal handgun meant that the Mexican was of relatively high importance. The firepower of the biker shouting orders was less impressive than his command over the remaining forces. Bolan wanted to talk to these two right away.

He brought up the Desert Eagle and fired a single .44 Magnum slug. Thirty yards away, up the stairs, the biker spilled onto the steps with tooth-breaking force. The Mexican stumbled behind him, cursing in Spanish as he tried to regain his footing.

Bolan spared a second round, this time targeting the gleaming gun in the Mexican gangster's hand. Fingers, metacarpal bones and the butt of the gold-finished Magnum all blew apart in a rain of gore, bone splinters, bent metal and chopped rubber. The Mexican drug lord howled in agony as his right hand was utterly destroyed by the same kinetic force that had crippled the Wizards gun thug.

Suddenly, without orders being snapped at them from on high, the Mexican gangsters and bikers halted. Even the paramilitary neo-Nazi guards had frozen at the sight of Carbonas and Duncan taken down.

"Get him!" the commander of the bikers bellowed.

Even as the first of the SS-tattooed guards turned to face the Executioner, Bolan acquired his head as a target and fired once. The 240-grain bullet impacted right in the split between the two halves of the racist thug's mustache. The resulting impact tore the skull off the man, sending his head bouncing in one direction, brain still trapped in a bowl of bone, and his body, lower jaw flapping as a geyser of grisly ejecta gushed upward, toppled sideways.

A biker roared in defiance, perhaps thinking that if all of the gunmen acted at once, they could rain hell upon Bolan, turning him into a perforated sack of chopped beef. Bolan whipped to the sound of his voice and put another brutal slug right at the bridge of the man's nose. The detonation of the biker's skull was not as dramatic as decapitation by single-shot, but the huge canyon carved by the Desert Eagle's bullet was still impressive, and far bloodier as pieces of brain and bone flew in a widening blossom of gore.

The Desert Eagle was half-empty, and the odds were still at least six to one. Bolan let the hand cannon lower, then pulled his Beretta 93-R machine pistol from its shoulder holster with his left hand. With its attached suppressor, fold-down lever and extended 20-round magazine, the Beretta pistol looked exactly like what it was, a hand-size machine pistol. The blunt suppressor was fat, giving the impression of a huge barrel, and the long magazine poking out of the butt also hinted at full-auto firepower.

The Executioner stomped into the open, both weapons ready to spit hot lead.

"Yeah. Get me!" Bolan bellowed. "Like that's worked for you guys before!"

Surrounded by bloody corpses, the smashed remains of a store, and the Challenger aflame from the damage it had taken from grenade and pre-planted high explosives, the remaining fighters stood, perhaps evaluating their position. Bolan was standing atop a mountain formed by crushed shelves, out in the open. His lower face was a greasy red mask where his nose flowed with blood. Bolan didn't know what kind of bruises or lacerations he had suffered in his brief brawl, but he knew the damage was mostly cosmetic. He'd recovered from his injuries in the crash and fight enough to inflict even more losses upon this group.

Whatever Bolan looked like to the gunmen—a battered fighter or a barbarian killing machine, the response of the gunmen was unanimous. They threw down their weapons and took off running out the entrance.

Anyone who'd showed an ounce of fight was already dead, except for the Wizards gun thug who crawled, trying to sit up and hold the massive automatic shotgun at the same time.

Bolan advanced to the stairs, climbing to face down the pair of wounded bosses that he now recognized from Stony Man's earlier photo upload.

The Mexican, Carbonas, clutched the stump of his right hand, watching as the Executioner climbed closer to them. Duncan, the Wizards gun thug, managed to lift the barrel of the powerful shotgun, but Bolan kicked it, stomping it to the floor and sending it out into the wreckage of the store where its 12-gauge bursts couldn't harm anyone.

"Let go of the gun," Bolan said.

Duncan raised both his hands, face gone pale and sweaty.

Carbonas spat. "Not me, mate!"

"Give me a reason not to," Bolan returned. He aimed the Beretta at Carbonas, and leveled the Desert Eagle at Duncan.

"We were about to load up and head to Miami," Duncan said quickly. "Carbonas got the call just before you showed up."

Bolan frowned. "Where in Miami?"

"Down to the river," Carbonas added. "We don't know where from there."

Bolan looked at the wreckage. "What exactly were you loading up?"

"Rockets," Duncan confessed.

Bolan nodded. "Miami River. Rocket launchers. Right."

Carbonas looked at the warrior who had taken on a deathly calm. "What are you going to do to us?"

"If you don't stay here until the cops arrive, I will find you," Bolan said. He gave Duncan's knee a light tap of his toe. "Then, crippled or not, you will die. Pray to spend the rest of your lives in jail."

With that, the Executioner turned. He hoped that Nappico could find them some transportation fast.

They had to get down to Miami as soon as humanly possible.

13

Brognola looked at the scene in the military surplus warehouse. The incinerated Dodge Challenger, which he could recognize by the grille badge and the rough shape of the charred shell, sat in the middle of the carnage, its top blown off. Dozens of corpses were strewed around, heads torn open by Magnum slugs, chests ruptured by full-auto blasts.

There were two survivors still on the scene, and a dozen weapons that had been thrown away by criminals terrified of what had struck them. Those who had decided to run, dropped to their knees and surrendered to cops as they arrived on scene, sirens blaring.

The head Fed found Bolan's machine pistol, half-empty, discarded, as it had snagged against collapsed shelves. Brognola wondered at the blood splattered all over the place, and thought that it could be his friend's, judging from where it had spilled and where the weapon had fallen.

"He must have been in a hurry," Buck Greene noted.

"Which means he got some information from those two out in the ambulances," Brognola returned. "How are they doing?"

"One's weak and delirious from blood loss. The other guy with the broken leg is unconscious—he's in shock," Greene returned. "We can get them back to health, but you're going to have to find out from Striker what's really going on."

"I figured that already," Brognola returned. "What about the delirious jerk?"

"His hand was torn apart by a single shot," Greene said. "We also found pieces of a wrecked Desert Eagle…not Striker's, unless he's currently using a pimp gun."

"So he took out the guy's weapon, too," Brognola mused. "Did he say anything?"

"Mentioned Miami several times," Greene told him. "Miami and river."

Brognola grimaced. "There's a lot of things along the Miami River that would be a tempting target. But that doesn't give us what Kilo and Tonne are really after."

There was a call from below. "Sirs! We've found something that you should really look at!"

Brognola and Greene didn't pause. They knew that if an agent were that nervous, it was truly something of note.

There, in crates loaded next to a truck, were the unmistakable tubes, complete with the bell-shaped bulges at the end, that signified a low-recoil, shoulder-fired missile launcher.

"Buck?" Brognola asked.

"Those are M-47 variants," Greene answered, taking a closer look. "These appear to be Super Dragons."

Brognola stepped closer, running his hand over one of the tubes. "What kind of punch can we expect from one of these?"

"These were meant to make up for shortcomings of the original M-47 Dragon. They can penetrate eighteen inches of armor plate," Greene replied. "And they have a range of nearly 5000 feet."

"A mile," Brognola mused, looking at them. "Eighteen inches of armor…"

"To be used against '90s-era tanks or bunkers. Trouble is, they didn't prove too popular. Still, during the Iran-Iraq war, they tore the hell out of all manner of Soviet tanks. They were good enough that Iran captured copies we'd lent to the Iraqi military and reverse engineered them," Greene said.

"Definitely not good news," Brognola grumbled. "You think one of these could take on a Coast Guard cutter?"

Greene's eyes widened. "They'd blow the hell out of an 87-footer, like the Dolphin based out of Miami."

Brognola ground his teeth. "There's, what, six or seven based south of Star Island?"

"Seven," Greene replied. "You think that Kilo and Tonne want to take on the U.S. Coast Guard?"

Brognola nodded. "One of the things that has really hurt all manner of smuggling into and out of Miami is the presence of strong maritime patrols. All right, check to see if there's listings of anything else here! I want to know just how much firepower these bastards have on hand!"

With that, Brognola pulled out his cell phone, dialing to reach Bolan.

IT WASN'T THE CHALLENGER, Bolan had to admit, but the Cadillac Coupe was pushing hard to race down Route 96 to see just what the hell was on tap for the Chief Dozen in Miami. For a car from the '80s, it was still smooth riding, having been tenderly cared for by the crew boss at the construction site. Nappico was behind the wheel while Bolan made certain that his scalp wouldn't come apart.

The bloody gash in the back of his skull was just a nasty split. At the beginning, Bolan took out a set of body trimmers from his war bag, meant especially for such a situation. Pressing the wound shut with his fingers, he removed his hair from around the scalp injury, taking care not to cause more damage to his skin. He poured a tube of antibiotic ointment into the injury, then taped the wound shut with athletic tape. It'd tug on his scalp, but with enough applications and a wrap-around, Bolan would be certain not to open it up again until he could get stitches.

Presently, with the Chief Dozen's Miami gun base equipped with deadly armor-piercing, bunker-destroying rockets, there were more important things than ugly scarring that could be covered by letting his hair grow out. The Executioner had secured himself against blood loss and infection, and he'd self-diagnosed himself as being free from concussion. He could fight, and that was what was necessary at the moment.

His cell phone vibrated, and Bolan answered it.

"Hal?"

"You knew I'd find that blowout and the missiles, right?" Brognola asked.

"Yes," Bolan answered. "Did you hear about the Miami River, as well?"

"Affirmative," Brognola shot back. "We're sending out a warning to the Coast Guard station. We're concerned because there are at least seven ships on duty there."

"You're surmising that there is going to be an assault on the Coast Guard craft stationed in Miami and Miami Beach," Bolan replied.

"You don't?" Brognola asked.

"It looks like a tempting target, but you know me. I'm seeing at least a dozen possibilities for the use of the abandoned police station," Bolan said.

"Abandoned Miami PD," Brognola murmured. "How long have you known about it?"

"I've only suspected," Bolan returned. "But things keep pointing to the river. Letting out onto the river really seems like a lightning rod for all of this. From there, there are several major parks full of tourists, and to the north of the river is the Miami federal courthouse—never mind all of downtown Miami packed along the banks."

"I simply assumed a Coast Guard assault because of the weapons and their earlier assault on the West Palm Beach courthouse," Brognola answered.

"It could be a combination. Lord knows that a violent attack at Lummus Park, Brickell and Brickell Key Park or Bayfront Park would pull in not just the Coast Guard, but Miami PD and your federal strike force," Bolan returned. "Anything going on at the Miami Convention Center?"

There was silence on the other end. Bolan had already called up the schedule for the convention center, but knew that Brognola, with his Justice Department ties, would know exactly what was up.

"The Federal Marshal auction," the big Fed murmured over the phone.

"Lots of law enforcement, lots of loot, and most importantly, a perfect place to spit in the eye of the federal government," Bolan said.

"But what makes you think this is their target?" Brognola asked.

"Because that is the one prize that will allow Kilo and Tonne to make a profit," Bolan returned. "Those two are cold-blooded killers, and they take delight in painful murder, but they are also looking to make some advances in their standings among the criminal community."

"So if they snatch up a fleet of SUVs and luxury cars, they'll control prices on the chopped-auto market against other gangs, or they could make themselves indispensable in any major transport deal," Brognola mused.

"That's my theory," Bolan said. "Otherwise, the Wizards and the Mexican cartels wouldn't give a bunch of island boys like Le Loupe Grotte the time of day, let alone the neo-Nazi thugs working with the Wizards out of the warehouse."

"Just how large a force do you see hitting the convention center?" Brognola asked. He grunted. "They're going to be moving auction vehicles into the center starting at eleven tonight."

Bolan wrapped a do-rag around his skull, so as to minimize additional pressure on the scalp bandage, but to protect it and keep its tape from unraveling A firm knot, and Bolan was set. "Which means that's when things would be the most vulnerable."

"The Marshals are spread thin, between here and the auction," Brognola returned. "We've got six hours…"

"If that's even the plan," Bolan replied.

"So what do we do until then?" Brognola asked.

"You get the Coast Guard and the Marshals to batten down the hatches and throw all the manpower you can into security," Bolan ordered.

"And you will hit the station house alone," Brognola said.

"No. Not alone," Bolan said.

Nappico glanced at him.

"I've got a partner of this outing. Together, we'll figure out what Kilo and Tonne are up to," Bolan explained. "And we'll take care of them before they can launch another attack."

"This is the one you were talking about," Brognola asked.

"He's got a lot to make up for," Bolan replied. "At least to himself. He had to make a choice that no human should have to make, let alone no cop or father."

Nappico's knuckles whitened on the wheel.

"He's ready. I'm always ready. This ends before the sun sets," Bolan promised.

"Godspeed, Striker," Brognola whispered, almost in prayer.

The Cadillac roared on as Bolan disconnected.

THE TWO MEN PULLED TO WITHIN a few blocks of the old station house. Nappico was out and checking his AR-15 carbine. It wasn't the multipurpose, twenty-first-century assault weapon that Bolan's Blackout was, but it could still fire a 5.56 mm cartridge that was brutally destructive at under 300 yards, even on single shot. With a red-dot sight, he had excellent first-shot-hit capability and rapid target acquisition without limiting his field of view. And as he'd proved before, he was quick on the trigger, so even though one shot was fired per trigger pull, he could crank off two or three rounds in a second, ripping open his targets.

Bolan's Blackout carbine was equally adept. The weapon had been set up as a designated marksman's rifle, but Bolan was just as sharp and quick on the draw as Nappico, able to put five rounds into a target before the man began to fall.

Even so, Bolan would have preferred something more ideal for a room sweeper, and he had that, as well. Duncan's USAS-12 was a brawny, powerful weapon, but as Bolan was trained in the use of a Squad Automatic Weapon such as the M-249 or the shoulder-firing M-60 light machine gun, this was no different. The Executioner had gathered up all of the magazines that Duncan had available, and they were all loaded with No. 4 buckshot rounds, launching a swarm of twenty-seven quarter-inch pellets at a velocity of just over 1300 feet per second. One-and-a-quarter ounces of pellets moving at that speed struck with the force of more than a ton of impact energy with all pellets striking home. Even if only sixty percent of the rounds hit center mass, the resultant carnage would be far worse than anything an AR could put out in rapid fire.

Nappico had a Remington 870 with a folding stock slung across his back, and he would be making use of the No. 4 buckshot, as well, springing forth, death by the ton of energy. Nappico would suffer more because his sleek, efficient pump gun didn't have the pure bulk or gas operation systems to absorb that kind of recoil, but then, neither did Nappico have to worry about a semi-auto jamming, or its unwieldiness in close quarters. Either way, the two men were armed to the teeth, Nappico supplementing his rifle and shotgun with his duty-issue USP .40 and its "nephew," a .40-caliber P-30 autopistol, matching Bolan's formidable pair of the Desert Eagle and Beretta 93-R.

Bolan also took the opportunity to jam some more gear into the backseat of the Cadillac, including a "Super Dragon" rocket launcher and a satchel of hand grenades, a mixture of MK-3 cylindrical concussion grenades and M-67 "baseball" fragmentation grenades. As there was nothing to suggest that Kilo and Tonne had anyone other than their fellow Chief Dozen members as prisoners, neither man had to worry about the consequences of unleashing a wave of shrapnel in a room full of hostages. Even so, the MK-3 concussion grenades were minimal fragmentation, producing powerful waves of force that stunned, blinded or even killed at close enough distances.

Bolan and the fallen cop split the supply of hand grenades between them, then set up their approach to the abandoned station house. Standing on the shore of the Miami River, they had a clear view to the back of the building.

"I'll make my way in close, first," Nappico said, securing his gear.

"Why?" Bolan asked.

"I'm less heavily loaded, and I don't know how to operate a shoulder-fired rocket launcher," Nappico answered. "You can use that thing to soften those bastards up, then hump the rest of the way in."

Bolan looked at his bulky USAS-12, then at Nappico's 870. He'd be tempted to trade, but the cop was right. The Haitians were cold-blooded murderers who needed to be put down as quickly and brutally as possible. That meant he'd have to open the battle with the M-47 Super Dragon, and he had the training and discipline with the older launcher so as to keep the brute on target even as it fired its 30-pound rocket.

Bolan also knew that he could race along the shore to the station house within the space of thirty seconds, even packing the rifle and his shotgun.

"I'll use the optics on my rifle and our com link to get you in as quietly and safely as possible," Bolan said. "You just need to make sure that there are only bad guys in place."

Nappico nodded. "I'm not going to blow off on a suicidal rampage in there."

"Never thought you were," Bolan answered. "You get killed early, you can't make sure that Kilo and Tonne pay for what they did to Liz."

Nappico swallowed. Bolan could see that he'd tasted bile with that statement, the memory of what happened to his partner. "You're right. You don't have to remind me."

Bolan took Nappico by the upper arm, looking into his eyes. "Listen, I've lost people I've loved. I've felt the guilt you have because I dragged them into my war. I've felt the anger that you have, the need to strike back."

Bolan let the fallen cop see what was in his soul, the pain, the scars, the everlasting nightmares. "Anger isn't going to get you through this. It'll provide that push, that little extra for when you don't think you can step farther, but you have to be alert. Thinking. You have to be able to put those emotions in a pocket until they're needed. Otherwise, it'll be like with Dominic."

"I hated him so much…but I felt sick hurting him," Nappico replied.

Bolan nodded. "When I was in sniper-scout school, I was told that any man could make one sniper shot in their life. The trick was to be able to do it again. Killing a person is hard."

"I was able to take out those gun thugs at the safehouse, and I put Sabrina down," Nappico said.

"And when it came time for more violence, it got to you," Bolan returned.

"Is that why you look so fearless and calm?" Nappico asked.

Bolan let go of his arm. "Going into battle without fear is like going into battle with one leg. Fear is your mind's way of making you alert. The thing is that you have to control that fear, control that anger. To the rest of the world, I might look like an emotionless monk, a living killing machine, but going totally numb is just as bad as giving in to fury."

Nappico took a deep breath. "Does the hurt and guilt ever go away?"

Bolan shook his head. "You just have to deal with it, and do everything you can to ease the pain of others. Me, it means taking on monsters like the Chief Dozen around the world."

"How long have you been going?" Nappico asked.

Bolan shook his head again. "I can't tell you. It's for your safety, should we get out of this."

"But you've been to Florida before. Plenty of times," Nappico said. His eyes narrowed. "But for some of those times, you weren't among friends."

"Not officially," Bolan returned. "You're not doing this as a penance, Tony. You're doing this to protect people, all of the men and women who could die if the Chief Dozen and Le Loupe Grotte achieve power."

"So you're stuck for the rest of your life," Nappico said.

Bolan grimaced at the description. "I'm not stuck. I choose to do this because I have the skills and the knowledge of where to apply them. I'm not paying penance anymore."

Bolan rested his hand on the broken cop's shoulder. "This

can be the forge that cleanses you of your sins. This isn't permission to subject yourself to more harm than necessary. This is all about getting the job done and doing far more good than harm. And even if that lofty abstract isn't enough, you need to be there for your family."

Nappico nodded. "All right. I'm in sync with the plan."

"You don't need to penetrate into the building if you don't have to, or if the defenses are too tight. But what you do need to do is make certain that there's no one we have to rescue before we hit them, all rockets blazing," Bolan said. "I'll take up position over there and be your eyes and ears."

"You've got X-ray vision on that scope?" Nappico asked.

"If I can't see it, perhaps I can call upon a higher power," Bolan said with a wink.

Nappico looked up into the sky, then smiled. "God or satellites, it don't matter."

Bolan smirked back. "Live large."

Nappico flashed his teeth in a cocksure rictus. "This is Miami law enforcement. We do that every damn day."

EMILE KILO WAS GROWING frustrated with his cell phone, but he restrained the urge to hurl it against the wall, then stomp on the broken pieces. For a cold-blooded murderer, he knew the value of restraint, especially since it took time to set up a new, clean burner. He looked over at his partner, Ian Tonne.

"We've finally got word on your woman," Kilo said.

"Yeah, I just got the call, too," Tonne answered. "Did you hear about our armory?"

Kilo's eyes narrowed. "I've been trying to get through to them. They should have phoned the moment they pulled out to come here."

Tonne shook his head. "We're not going to get the extra firepower in."

Kilo shuddered, containing an eruption of fury that threatened to leave him in a fit of screaming, and shooting the messenger. Rather than go berserk, he grit his teeth and let off steam in a slow, long exhalation. "Let me guess, it wasn't the cops."

"They showed up after someone rammed a big black muscle car through the front," Tonne returned. "There was only one man in the car, and he didn't stop, even after they put a grenade into the hood of that car. He just got out and continued slaughtering men. Duncan and Carbonas were left behind when this big bastard told them that they wouldn't stand a chance against him."

Kilo frowned. "You mean, just one guy has been doing all this?"

"That's what the survivors said. Most of them were picked up by the Feds as they rushed in," Tonne told him.

Kilo rubbed his goateed chin, thumb scraping the thick nap of his neatly trimmed beard. "One guy, killing everyone in his path."

"I think it's the Soldier, too," Tonne said.

Kilo shook his head. "That guy is a fantasy. A myth. A story that mob bosses tell their children to keep them in line." He affected a semblance of a famous movie mobster, puffing out his cheeks and speaking softly. "'The Man in Black is going to come get you if you fuck up, son…'"

Tonne grimaced. "Yeah. But what about Big Freddy, back home? He was calling in muscle to deal with the same kind of fucker. And what happens? He doesn't end up in jail, but pieces of his shark-chewed body end up washing up along miles of beach."

"Superstition," Kilo murmured, but his conviction was waning.

"So what do we do? Fold and make like we are cowards?" Kilo asked. "We've put a lot on the line, Ian."

"Em, I'm just saying that we need to steel up and get ready for a hurricane," Tonne answered. "Because when this Black Bastard hits, he's a goddamn force of nature."

Kilo grumbled, but his partner had a point. "Okay. So, we won't have the same overwhelming firepower we had at the

West Palm courthouse, but we've still got some shoulder-fired rockets and grenade launchers, and plenty of assault rifles. The auction shouldn't be too much of a hard nut to crack."

"We'll figure that out later," Tonne said.

Kilo looked at him quizzically. "What makes you think he's on us?"

"Because it only takes a half hour to get from there to here, obeying traffic laws," Tonne answered. "And he's definitely going to be here if he found out where those missiles were going."

"You think he's that good," Kilo said.

"Oh, let's underestimate the bastard who took out the hit team sent to get Selena and Dr. Death, wrecked our hotel and an arms warehouse loaded with gunmen," Tonne mocked nasally. "And don't forget that he was there to make sure every single man was dead at Togor, both assault and defense."

Kilo frowned. He lifted a finger. "All right, but you talk to me like I'm a goddamned idiot again, I will cut your tongue out!"

Tonne grimaced. "Sorry, brother."

Kilo sighed. "Okay, we assume that this guy *is* a walking devil. So what do we do?"

Tonne nodded toward the cells. "We've gotten what we could from them."

"Arm men we've beaten and tortured?" Kilo asked. "Do you want a bullet in your head?"

Tonne shook his head. "Not those idiots. Some of them can barely walk."

"The cop's daughter," Kilo muttered.

"We bring her out and keep her with us," Tonne said. "That should give us some shielding."

"If it's not enough?" Kilo asked.

"We still have her getting hit before we do, buying at least a few seconds," Tonne answered. "Come on. Get a gun, and let's get our men ready to fight."

Kilo nodded. Hell was on its way, and there could be nothing left to chance if they wanted to see another sunset.

14

Anthony Nappico kept himself in the water as he approached the dock the station house had used for its river patrol craft. Against the waves, his dark hair and clothes were invisible. He didn't worry about his guns, either. The HK pistols were as close to bricks as possible, in fact, they were tougher than bricks. He couldn't get one of the handguns to jam or break, even with the hottest ammunition. The rifle was also good for brief dips in the Miami River, and the Remington 870, loaded with plastic-hulled shells, was also immune to the elements.

It was going to be a submerged assault.

"Hold," Cooper's voice whispered in his ear.

The big, brawny warrior spoke softly, so as not to startle him, causing a stealth-destroying flinch. Cooper had obviously worked overwatch before, but that was a given with his mention of being a sniper scout. The elite riflemen of the Army and the Marines were not just tasked with high-value targets or enemy harassment—they were specifically utilized as the most capable form of forward observation available to ground troops. Good radio discipline and communication were vital for such men. Nappico followed Cooper's orders, remaining still—so motionless, in fact, that he could have been mistaken for a piece of flotsam in the water, breathing only when a wave created a depression below his nose and mouth, rather than moving himself to suck down air.

"Go," the warrior ordered. With that, Nappico reached up,

grabbed the dock and hauled himself onto the deck, rolling behind spools of mooring rope.

It was from this position that Nappico could see two guards, their backs to him at present.

"Leave the rifle and shotgun right there. I don't want you in the building when I start," Cooper told him. "You'll move faster without all that."

Nappico stripped off his long weapons and set his bandoleers next to them. "What now?"

"I see an entrance open and unattended," he told him. "Satellite gives you two minutes to get there."

"Take all of it?"

"Get there in thirty," Cooper whispered.

With that, Nappico dashed swiftly up to where he'd been told to go, HK P-30 drawn and clasped firmly in both hands. He'd affixed a suppressor to the threaded barrel provided with the handgun so that if he did have to shoot, he wouldn't alert the whole station house. Still, even with subsonic 180-grain hollow-nosed slugs, the .40's report would be loud enough to alert some of the Haitians on site. He kept his finger off the trigger so as not to accidentally trip an errant round, though he'd cocked the hammer.

Nappico didn't even have the excuse of being drenched to the skin from his immersion in the river to shrug off that he was nervous. He would have been sweating like a pig, and he was surprised that he wasn't shaking hard enough to have shook himself dry like a shaggy dog. Cooper was right about the feeling of terror being your worst enemy, and his fear was as strong as his desire to get revenge.

He kept his back teeth clenched together, fighting off his emotions, mastering his body. He concentrated on what was important. He focused on that, honing his heart and mind into something that would not be swayed or bent by outside forces. Nappico kept his eyes and ears sharp, pausing when Bolan gave him the order to hold.

That's when he wondered just how much his emotional state could take.

Then he saw them—Kilo and Tonne. And between them was a familiar, slender figure.

"Oh, God," Nappico whispered.

"Who do they have, Tony?" Cooper asked, his tone irresistible.

"Jessie. My daughter. Those two butchers are…"

"Tony, we need you calm," Cooper ordered. He spoke up, as if he was putting all of his power and authority into the command. Somehow, that was enough. It was the anchor that kept Nappico from being washed away by a tidal wave of dread and dismay.

"Call my wife," Nappico whispered. "Get in touch with her. Find out…"

"Your daughter would have been at school today," Bolan replied. "They didn't have to go to your house."

"Just find out…"

"I am," the answer came. Nappico could sense some annoyance on the warrior's part, and he immediately felt apologetic, then realized that it was probably all part of Cooper's plan to get his mind off the deadly peril his child was in.

Nappico pressed the decocking button on the back of the P-30's slide, lowering the hammer. He wanted to make sure he didn't make it easy to pull the trigger and send a round snapping into the floor. If the two murderous mobsters felt as if they were under attack, there was a good chance that they'd use Jessie as a living shield.

Nappico didn't want to endanger Jessie any more than necessary. She was already in the lion's den, but she wasn't seized in their claws. She could get out of this without a mark.

If he remained as cool and collected as the warrior who'd been dragging him around for the past twenty hours.

Twenty hours, he mused. The previous night he had been in a bottle, pushing poison down his throat, ready to die. In this hour, he was ready to charge a dozen guns just to keep Jessie alive.

Nappico wiped the corner of his eye with the back of his hand. He grimaced. Waiting for Cooper was akin to watching a glacier move. But he was more upset with his own impatience, so he forced himself to keep his ears and eyes keen for anyone approaching. If a guard stumbled upon him, he'd end up in a brawl, or have to shoot, and once more, Jessie would end up hurt.

Bolan's voice entered his ear. "Dolores, Javier and Julie are all okay and accounted for. They snagged Jessie at school. I'm sorry that she's in this mix."

"You get her out," Nappico returned. "We can't use that fucking rocket launcher. And shotguns are bad, bad juju for hostage situations."

"Not necessarily, but I'm getting down there, ASAP," Bolan answered. "I'm leaving my USAS behind. I'll bring you your carbine."

"You're going to use the 870?" Nappico asked.

"Not when Jessie is in the picture," Bolan answered.

"Fair enough," Nappico said. "Get her fast."

There was no answer. The Executioner was on his way. Until then, Nappico had to watch his own six. He retreated to the shadows, a worried gaze locked on his daughter between two bloody madmen.

BOLAN HURLED BOTH THE USAS-12 and M-47 rocket into the Miami River. Brognola could have divers recover the weaponry later, but he wasn't going to be responsible for allowing an auto-shotgun and an anti-tank missile to fall into the hands of kids hanging around the shore. He hit the quick detach on the Blackout rifle's suppressor, set the selector switch to full-auto and took off into a lightning-fast run.

He was glad that someone was keeping an eye on the helpless. It had been Perez and Montenegro who had called in to Stony Man Farm when they'd checked on Nappico's family after double-checking on Montoya's surviving family. It had been a routine lunchtime stop for the two men when they'd learned that someone very similar to Montenegro in appearance had visited, identifying himself as the officer, and spirited away Jessie Nappico under the illusion of authority.

It wasn't a screwup on the school's part. It was simply reflective of just how devious and clever the Kiloton team was. They'd taken note of the possible law-enforcement involvement in Miami, picked a cop who one of their own could pass for, and sent him to grab a hostage, just in case.

The Executioner didn't have an ounce of respect for his enemy's methods, but he had to admit that if they were that sharp and on the ball, then they must have all manner of deadly traps. As it was, he counted forty men inside the station house, according to the infrared satellite imagery obtained by the Farm. That wasn't counting the ten men sprawled out in the holding cells, kept under lock and key.

Those men were the Chief Dozen, the ten captured Loupes who had been broken out two days ago. The Farm's infrared imagery couldn't give precise diagnoses of the sprawled men, but their lack of movement and body positions were all too indicative of brutal beatings and other means of torture.

Kilo and Tonne were on a rampage against their former comrades as well as their competition and persecutors in southern Florida. The two criminal masterminds had shown exactly how ruthless they were, and how much power they intended to unleash in their bid for criminal mastery. It hadn't been enough, before their apparent deaths, that they'd engaged in a running assault rifle battle in the middle of a crowded West Palm Beach mall. They had to throw heavy artillery at law enforcement, send armored vehicles to smash their competition, and then snatch a profit from a bloodied Marshall's auction. These two intended to return to the era when gangsters were far better armed than law enforcement, feared no one and unleashed bloody hell against their foes.

If these two gangsters managed a coup such as this, right down to being able to blow holes in Coast Guard cutters, it would have made the early part of the twentieth century seem like an era of peace and prosperity. Instead of BARs and Thompson submachine guns, Kilo and Tonne were set to raise the bar with high explosives capable of killing everyone on the floor of a building or to blow a bank vault off its hinges.

As it was, Bolan had cut them off from not only the Syndicate's storehouse of contraband weaponry, but also from their anti-tank rockets back in West Palm. It was only a setback. There was more firepower on the scene—enough to make a desperate stab at the Miami Convention Center and kill dozens of lawmen.

As Bolan approached the dock, he slowed. He'd been concentrating too far ahead, anticipating a wave of lawlessness that would erupt in the wake of the Haitians' coup in Miami. He had to deal with those two, and their forty hard men. His brow furrowed with concentration, and he knew that there was going to be one gambit that would give him a shred of an advantage.

"Tony, this isn't going to be easy," Bolan whispered as he waded through the water, approaching the point where the cop had left his weaponry behind.

"No shit," Nappico returned. "What are you warning me about?"

"I'm going to play a gambit here," Bolan said. "Don't freak when you hear one of my concussion grenades pop."

"Oh, dear fuck," Nappico gurgled, sounding as if he were trying to fight the bile back down his throat. "You're going to bring them to you."

"You're a smart man, Tony," Bolan said. "I'm going to give you an unmistakable signal when I want you to throw your concussion grenades. That should separate Kilo and Tonne from Jessie."

"And if she gets hurt?" Nappico asked.

"If she's outside, don't throw it inside of fifteen feet of them. If inside, throw it in the room next to them," Bolan said. "The pressure won't have an effect on them, but it'll feel like someone hit the building with a bomb."

"That's your plan?" Nappico asked.

"You'll get it when I show my hand," Bolan said.

With that, Bolan hurled one of his MK-3s high into the air. The concussion grenade went off with a clap of thunder that shook the air, then he scooped up Nappico's shotgun and rifle, adding that gear to his own. Luckily, Nappico had been keen enough not to dump his grenades behind with his guns and ammunition.

The concussion grenade blew in midair, creating a loud boom as it dissolved into a cloud of smoke.

With that, a dozen men rushed into the open and saw the Executioner standing at the end of the dock, an M-16 in each hand, a loose cigarette from one of the waterproof pockets on his harness dangling unlit from his lips. His jaw was bloodstained and blackened with stubble, and what was left of his hair was tucked underneath a do-rag. He took a cocksure stance.

For the Haitians, Mexicans and bikers in assembly, it was an odd, jarring sight. No one would have announced their presence in a thunderclap, and then stood like a target for a firing squad, looking like something out of a bad '80s action movie.

"I want to talk to Kilo and Tonne!" he bellowed.

Though he looked like a sitting duck, the Executioner had picked his spot well. He was standing at the edge of the dock, and he not only had large spools of abandoned mooring rope as cover, but all he had to do was step back and he would drop beneath the heavy timbers of the platform and into the water. The Loupes, Cartel gun thugs and Wizards outlaws could shoot at him all they wanted, but there was going to be no way that they would get him. Any attack they made from this point on would force them into the open, striking from two channels that Bolan could quickly cover and make inhospitable by fields of withering fire.

One of the men ran inside. It was a Haitian, chosen because the others didn't want to be the bringer of bad news to Kiloton. Bolan kept his ground.

"Who the hell are you?" a biker snapped in defiance, trying to look tough, yet he stayed where he could duck behind a wall.

"I'm the bastard who's been kicking your ass for the past day!" Bolan answered. "Who else is going to walk up and request a little talk?"

There was no response, but nervous glances were exchanged.

"What makes you think you can step up to our crew?" a Mexican shouted. His shotgun was clenched in white-knuckled fists.

Bolan turned and glared at the man, derision seeping off him as he let the cigarette bob between his lips. The cancer stick was a prop, kept on hand because it could be used for a fuse, to calm a rescued ally or to help light a campfire. He'd given up smoking long ago, but in his times undercover, Bolan knew that a properly "worn" cigarette was far more expressive than words. It had been shown by movie actors from spaghetti Westerns to Hong Kong bullet ballets to be a mark of a tough, hard man who didn't care. His loose, bored stance, the firepower he wore, and the unlit cigarette all added to an image intended to intimidate.

"Look, I didn't come to talk to the rent-a-guns. You should be glad I came spitting words, not lead," he said.

Bolan heard a snort on the other end of his radio contact. Nappico was amused, and by that factor, he could tell that the Kiloton and their friends were in a tizzy of confusion and fear.

"Kilo and Tonne left someone with Jessie," Nappico whispered. "They're coming out to see you. They're acting like you walked across the water."

Bolan grunted an assent, too low for the men at the back of the building to hear.

With that, the pair of Haitian gang bosses appeared. They were strapped, but to their credit, they kept their faces grim and tight, despite an initial flash of fear and recognition.

"Who are you, boss?" one of the two bosses—Bolan recognized him from his rap sheet as Tonne—asked.

"What matters is who you two are," Bolan responded. "Are you going to be smart and walk away from this city? Or are you just dead men walking?"

"Oh! I see who he is." Kilo spoke up. He was starting to laugh. "He's a goddamned retard who thinks that we're going to fold just because he made a couple of impressive splashes over the past day or so."

Bolan nodded. "Now, I'm not saying the Feds aren't going to be coming after you, but they're sure as hell not going to bring a ton of murder down on your heads."

"So what? One joke of a man thinks he can come here looking like a Terminator and spook us?" Tonne asked. He licked his lips, a nervous flinch that showed just how aware of their situation they were. This had to be a trick, and every instinct these men had demanded that they open fire and not stop until Bolan's body was reduced to a fine mist of blood droplets and bone splinters.

"Spook you," Bolan repeated. "So, the hotel was just nothing. Togor was a little fright."

Kilo and Tonne resisted looking at each other. But their entourage and the guards who'd been here since the first concussion grenade had brought them out into the open were all exchanging nervous glances and hushed, quick questions.

"What's your offer?" Kilo asked.

"You give up the cop's daughter, Jessie, then take your boats back to Haiti, back to your cousin's hillbilly shed, back to Tijuana or wherever you were born," Bolan said. "If you do that, I won't chase all of you down and kill you."

He grit his teeth with the last sentence, the cigarette suddenly erect and still as he spoke in a harsh rasp.

Kilo managed another laugh. His hand, however, was wrapped so tight around the handle of his assault rifle that Bolan was certain the skin on the man's fingers would split from the tension. "How about I just shoot you right now?"

"Look at the guns here. You're outnumbered, and you're surrounded!" Tonne said. He'd stepped away from Kilo. With that, the gunmen started to shift. They were moving so that they wouldn't be hit by a single spray of autofire.

"You don't think I showed up without some preparation, do you?" Bolan asked.

As soon as he'd mentioned Jessie, Bolan had heard Nappico

move, rising from his hiding spot. Even as he spoke with the Haitians and their minions, he could imagine the cop exploding into action. With the guards' attention all focused on the Executioner, on the standoff at the dock, they wouldn't be expecting a lone man inside their quarters.

Hopefully the suppressor on the P-30 would work well enough that Nappico wouldn't be heard outside. Bolan envisioned Nappico raising the handgun, hammer thumbed back so that he only had to fight a four-pound trigger to put his silenced rounds on the sentry making certain Jessie wasn't running anywhere.

One .40-caliber hollowpoint would go directly to center mass. A second would join it soon afterward. And these bullets would hit the hostage holder between his shoulder blades, the massive 180-grain slugs striking spinal column, shattering bone and severing the central nerve trunk line that would keep the man standing.

There'd be a yelp of surprise. A moment of fear as her father, looking like crap and still damp from his dip in the Miami River, approached Jessie, taking her by the wrist. Bolan could almost see their plan unfold.

"Got her," Nappico whispered, right on time. He sounded rattled, nervous, but the cop kept radio discipline.

"Preparations?" Tonne finally asked, bringing his rifle up to low ready. "What? You leave bombs all over this station house that we ain't found?"

"Your funeral," Bolan said. He took a giant step back, letting Nappico's carbine drop from one hand, triggering the Blackout on full-auto. In the instant before Bolan dropped below the dock, he sliced off half a dozen bullets in Tonne's general direction.

In response, everyone out back opened fire at the same moment. The roar of autofire was deafening, and even as Bolan knifed into the Miami River feet-first, he could see the timbers of the pier exploding into sawdust under a wave of bullets from dozens of weapons.

The water closed over Bolan's head, but his mental timer was still counting another second before the first of the concussion grenades went off.

That gave him a moment before he kicked to the surface, advancing out of the waters of the Miami River, Blackout shouldered, water sloughing off it thanks to combat tolerances that resisted jamming from dirt, mud and other debris. The first grenade thundered, interrupting the rainstorm of fire and vengeance launched by the criminal forces.

Instants later a second blast rocked the air and suddenly the gunfire stopped cold.

With the distraction of the two explosions, the Executioner swept around one side of the dock, triggering the Blackout with another burst, his second salvo in this fight, striking a biker in the jaw and peeling his head from his shoulders.

It was time for Kiloton to face a real living weapon.

Bolan was going to make good on his promise to kill every last one of the armed thugs.

15

Jessie watched her father pull the pin on a third fearsome-looking cylinder, then pressed her fingers tighter to her ears as he hurled it down the hallway to the back of the building. The resultant explosion didn't sound or feel as bad as the previous two, but that might have been because she was growing used to the shock waves, or that her dad had pushed his daughter farther from the conflict.

He was in retreat, and he was speaking to someone on a hands-free microphone and earpiece set. And when he moved, he held her tight to his side, a big, brutal-looking rifle clamped in one fist.

"Daddy?" she sputtered, not sure of what was going on. One moment she'd been surrounded by heavily armed thugs and the next, her father appeared, almost magically in the abandoned building, killing the one remaining guard holding her captive.

"Just keep moving ahead, baby," Nappico told her. "We're not out of this yet."

"Oh, Daddy," Jessie gasped. She immediately felt stupid, terribly clichéd, but there was nothing else she could think to say. People didn't just find themselves kidnapped or rescued, they didn't end up in the middle of such violence. Jessie had nothing to base any responses on.

All she could do was put one foot in front of the other, flinching as her dad spun and opened fire with that powerful automatic weapon, spraying bullets at the gunmen who were coming in through the door he'd hurled those grenades through. She ran, knowing that her dad was back there, fighting for her life.

Gunfire rattled long and hard, making her ears ache and skull throb from intense pressure put out by her father's muzzle blast. Jessie saw the front doors of the police station, and she sped up, knowing that freedom wasn't far away.

Then she noticed that the doors were boarded shut.

The only way out now seemed to be right back through an army of angry mobsters and bikers.

"Daddy!" Jessie shouted. "The door's blocked!"

"Take the stairs!" her dad answered. "To your right!"

Bullets smashed the wall over Jessie's head and she ducked, but headed for the flight of stairs her father had indicated.

She hoped he knew what he was doing.

IAN TONNE WAS GLAD HE'D THROWN on a bulletproof vest, because when the lone gunman opened fire, even though he looked like he wasn't aiming, Tonne caught two .300 Blackout slugs in his chest, and another bullet sliced through his unprotected biceps, forcing him to drop his own rifle. The impact spun him, dropping him to one knee.

That was when the air split with the chatter of full-auto mayhem all around him. Tonne grimaced, clamping his hand over the wounded arm, trying to think of what he had on him that could be used as a bandage. He looked at the door back into the police station, and figured that he could get inside and obtain some first aid there.

He took two steps toward the entrance, then noticed a canister bounce on the ground.

Tonne recognized a concussion grenade. He also realized that if he stayed where he stood, he would be seriously injured by the explosion. Without regard for his injured arm, Tonne turned back and jumped over the low wall where he'd taken fire. No one was shooting back, just his men cutting loose, all guns blazing, so that even Tonne's shouted warning of a grenade went unheard.

Then the thunderous rain of lead was punctuated by the unmistakable exclamation point of the MK-3 concussion grenade detonating. Smoke filled the air, and guns dropped from nerveless hands. The shock wave struck the riflemen hard enough to disarm them, stunning the group as they caught the blast right in their backs.

Tonne struggled to his feet, losing his footing more than once as he tried to support his weight with his injured arm. Only pure luck had kept the round from smashing the bone beneath the muscle, so he could at least move the limb around, but holding himself up was an agonizing proposition. He reached down and grabbed his sidearm, transferring it to his uninjured hand when even holding it up was painful.

"Get out of there!" Tonne shouted. A couple men, still able to hold on to their guns, crawled out from cover and into the open.

"He dropped into the river!" one of the Wizards riflemen said. "He's in the water!"

Tonne grimaced, but the biker rushed off toward the dock. "I should have just shot the bastard…"

"He was a sitting target," one of his fellow Loupes said. The guy tore a do-rag in two and wound it around Tonne's injury as an improvised bandage. "We didn't think he could…"

Another detonation split the air and one man fell lifeless to the ground. The back of his skull sported a metal cylinder—the detonator of a less-than-lethal hand grenade, Tonne could tell. He'd killed a man with one before, and was surprised at the sheer power and destruction of the detonator's impact. Then he spotted Kilo stumbling, bouncing off walls, blinded and deafened.

Suddenly, gunfire spit anew, and Tonne watched the biker who'd rushed toward the river lose his head, a burst of gunfire splitting his skull apart.

"Don't go to him! Get back inside!" Tonne ordered.

He thought about grabbing Kilo, but his partner was dazed, less than useless as he had dropped his weapon, hands clamped over ruptured eardrums. He could barely stand, thanks to the disruption of the balance organs in his ears.

Tonne and his five barely capable gunmen moved toward an alternate door and shuffled inside even as a third mighty detonation shook the air.

The lone gunman wasn't alone. He had sneaked someone inside.

No wonder he had spoken of taking precautions. It was time to do or die. And Tonne intended to survive, no matter who he had to run over.

THE EXECUTIONER SPOTTED an injured Tonne leave the dock area, cutting through another door. He was tempted to send a few rounds after the Haitian murderer, but there were other men who either had shaken off a pair of concussion grenades, or were just not giving a damn that their brains were rattled as they aimed their rifles at him. Still, Bolan had the advantage of the slope of the shore for cover, and he saw his foes before they could figure out where he was coming from.

The Blackout spat another burst, cutting off an enemy shooter who was bleeding profusely from his ears. The MK-3's were devastating weapons in enclosed areas, and the doorway that Nappico had thrown them through created a perfect funnel for venting intense pressure against the men gathered out back. The rifleman he'd just taken out, the shoulders of his white-linen suit drenched in blood, folded over as 125-grain bullets stitched a line across his belly, cutting him in two.

Bolan fired two more bursts, taking out other healthy targets when he heard a summons over his earpiece.

"We're heading to the second floor. Inside's getting hot and the front door is locked," Nappico said quickly.

"Tonne and a bunch of shooters are headed your way," Bolan warned back, triggering a fourth burst that cored a Haitian gun thug through the breastbone. The man flopped backward, heart destroyed by a trio of high powered bullets. There were others, their brains still too scrambled to do more than hobble or struggle to their feet.

Bolan saw Kilo bouncing back and forth, unable to keep

his balance as he clutched his ears in agony. The Executioner sprinted to the low wall that Kilo was behind, vaulted it and slammed both of his combat boots into the Chief Dozen assassin's side. The Haitian bounced hard against the wall with a grunt, his eyes suddenly gaining focus as he spotted the man who had been plaguing his rampage for two days.

Anger and recognition didn't do much for Kilo; he was slow, clumsy. Bolan laid him out with a hard swipe of his rifle's buttstock to the jaw. Bone shattered like glass, teeth flying from the impact. Emile Kilo crashed to the floor, blood bubbling from between his lips. There would be time to properly execute Kilo's sentence when the rest of the assembled army was put away for good.

Bolan no longer had his CPDA giving him a layout of the scene, but he knew that the fifteen men who'd assembled here at the back were only a third or so of the force that Kilo and Tonne had assembled. For the time being, the unconscious Haitian wasn't going anywhere. And even if he did, he was deaf and barely able to talk.

He couldn't get far.

The Executioner heard the roar of autofire inside. That had to have been Nappico defending himself and his daughter. Luckily, Bolan had his satchel of grenades with him, drawing out a Type 67 and popping its pin.

He saw down the hallway to the lobby, a group of shooters crouched just out of sight of the stairs, he presumed by his memorization of the station's layout. Sure enough, bullets snapped into the ground. Bolan released the safety spoon, let the grenade cook a few seconds, then rolled it right toward the clot of gunmen. A biker turned at the sound of the steel-shelled fragmentation grenade bouncing off the floor and started to form the first words of a warning.

It was too late. After that first bounce, the fragger went off with an earthshaking explosion. The lethal radius of the fragmentation grenade was fifteen feet, and there wasn't a single gunman who was outside of that perimeter. Razor-sharp bits of wire and broken casing whipped through flesh and bone. There were men who were wearing vests, which allowed their torsos to survive the mangling wave of destruction, but their arms and legs were perforated, slashed to tatters.

Even so, there were four of the seven men still standing, each in varying degrees of ability to fight, though none of them was looking anywhere near him.

Bolan reloaded the Blackout, shouldered his rifle, and triggered off a series of single shots that cracked skulls and scrambled brains, putting the wounded out of their misery. This was going to be a slaughter, and he didn't care to allow men to go through the slow agony of bleeding to death.

He flicked the rifle back to full-auto, looking for signs of other gangsters. He counted that he'd brought down eleven so far, with Kilo and another four too battered by concussion grenades to contribute to this battle yet. That was fifteen, and he threw in the guard that Nappico killed, calling this a forty-percent reduction in the defensive force on the site.

That might have been great news, but there were still twenty-four armed killers up and ready to fight.

"Where are you holed up?" Bolan asked.

"Second-floor interrogation room," Nappico answered over the radio. "I've got Billy Skruggs from the Chief Dozen in here. He's cuffed, and beat all to hell."

Bolan went over the prosecution files in his mind. Skruggs wasn't one of the witnesses the district attorney had flipped. Either way, Skruggs was responsible for dozens of murders on his own time.

"Try not to make any noise. If Skruggs looks like he'll speak up, end him," Bolan said.

There was a pause. "I've got a knife to take him down."

"Hold down tight," Bolan said. "I've got work to do."

There was movement down a hall branching off an intersection he'd passed to put mercy rounds into the grenade-wounded gunners. Bolan turned and transitioned to the Remington shotgun. He was going to use that, because at this range, he could be assured of one-hit kills with his payloads. The No. 4 Buck was the same diameter as the rifle rounds he generally used in the ARs, and each shot shell held almost a full magazine's worth of the pellets.

When the first two men, Haitian gunmen each packing their own shotguns, appeared, the Executioner triggered the big Remington, its 12-gauge payload spreading out a ton of kinetic energy across the pair before they even realized he was there. Blasted off their feet, Bolan racked the slide, keeping the gold bead front sight aimed at the hallway.

A biker only barely showed himself around the corner, crouched low and aiming his own rifle at the spot where he assumed Bolan was. Bolan fired so that the No. 4 buck would skip along the wall, .24-caliber pellets slicing into the side of the biker's head, his shoulder and his assault rifle, ripping them all out into the intersection. The blast was brutal, and where the pellets struck, they'd peeled away flesh and cracked bone, or mangled the furniture and magazine of the assault rifle.

With that response and three already down, dead or dying, Bolan could hear the enemy withdrawing. Just to cover their retreat, a storm of bullets chopped at the buckshot-pocked wall where the biker died. Bolan took that opportunity to thumb fresh shells into the tube magazine, getting ready in case this were a feint. He gripped the Remington in one hand, dug in for a MK-3 grenade, and flipped out the cotter pin with his thumb. Safety lever popping, Bolan took a half step to the center of the hall and hurled it toward the far wall of the intersection.

The plastic canister bounced off that corner and shot down the hallway where the enemy gunners had retreated. Even as he made certain that the grenade rebounded in the direction he wanted it to go, Bolan took off. Real counterterror professionals moved so that they entered a concussed room "on the bang." Waiting a moment for the blast to clear would only allow the enemy more time to recover their senses.

Bolan was two feet from the intersection when the MK-3 detonated, and he could feel the air shoved hard into his face like a hard breeze. On the other side of the corner, the shock waves and intense pressure released by the concussion grenade would be far more powerful and mind-numbing. The Executioner rounded the corner, swung up his shotgun and saw that two of the enemy gunners, Mexican cartel soldiers, were still standing.

Boom! A 12-gauge shell thumped, and one of the Mexicans disappeared, slapped to the floor by a deadly storm of pellets that punched through flesh and bone as if they were made of clay and dry twigs. Bolan racked the slide, working it hard and fast so he didn't short stroke the shotgun and make it jam. Sure enough, Bolan's swift and sure pump put another live shell under the firing pin and the warrior slammed out another shotgun blast, this one punching the other rifle-armed killer just above the sternum.

This impact only sent the Cartel fighter staggering back. He was wearing body armor, so the pellets wouldn't have gotten to vital organs, ballistic polymers robbing the double O buck of their penetration power. Even so, the kinetic energy transfer staggered Bolan's target enough that he could work the slide a second time and aim higher. This time, the volley of .24-caliber projectiles was at head level, many of them striking the throat and shoulders of his enemy and reducing his face to a pulpy, spongy mass of blood and bone splinters.

Three rounds down, and the other gunmen were on the floor, twisting and rolling to try to get a shot at the Executioner. One fired his pistol, a thunderous roar blasting from the Magnum's muzzle, but instead of punching through to Bolan, the grounded shooter accidentally struck one of his allies in the back of his head. Bolan thanked the Magnum packer for doing his work for him with a pump and a squeeze of the Remington's trigger. At the range of only thirty feet, the swarm of double O buck slammed into the man, the pattern dropping off as it flowed against the man's crotch, up through his groin and belly, punching deep under his sternal notch and through his heart and diaphragm.

Four down, but there were another three killers scrambling. One of the men dragged a corpse across his chest, using the body as a shield, but Bolan let the Remington drop on its sling and whipped out the mighty Desert Eagle. Since he was going on an assault inside a building, he'd eschewed the Glaser Safety rounds, replacing them with flat-nosed .305-grain jacketed semi-wadcutters. The broad plate tips of those Magnum rockets provided plenty of contact area to damage an enemy's tissue, but had more than sufficient mass to not be stopped by even solid bone.

With a half ton of kinetic energy behind the first shot, Bolan punched through the lifeless gunman and reached the biker thug behind him. Bolan tapped in a second round, just to make certain, and those two doses of bear-hunting medicine were more than sufficient to end this particular exchange.

Another was halfway to his feet, scooping up his rifle. Bolan adjusted his aim and put another shot into the bridge of the Haitian's nose. The impact produced a small hole in the center of the man's face, but the back of his skull opened up in wide, bloody petals, vomiting brains in a mist of gore.

The last of the enemy shooters hurled his gun away from him, covering up his head and crying in dismay. Bolan walked to him, looking down at the frightened fool who had bitten off far more than he could chew.

"Get up and get away from these weapons," Bolan ordered. The biker peered between his forearms. Bolan had him under the muzzle of the hand cannon, and he knew that the Desert Eagle was designed to look impressive. It was a wide-bottomed pyramid with a cavernous hole at the top, resembling, for all the world, the front of a tank or an ice cutter.

"What?"

"Run away. Unarmed," Bolan repeated. "Or you can die here."

With the boneless ease of a snake, the Wizard outlaw was on his feet, hightailing it to the back of the building, toward the dock, one of the sure ways out of this slaughterhouse that used to be a police station.

Unfortunately for the biker thug, but fortunate for Bolan, he heard the chatter of gunfire as the man reached the back hall.

"Tonne! Tonne! Where the fuck did you go?" Kilo shouted, lisping and spitting through lost teeth.

The odds were turning back against the Executioner, but he took out another MK-3 grenade out and whipped it in the direction of the Haitian crook's voice. He turned and tore back to the lobby and up the stairs. Even as he advanced up the steps, he fed the partially spent Desert Eagle, holstered it, then stuffed fresh shells into the breech of the Remington. He was done with all of this by the time he reached the top of the stairs where he then scanned for enemy gunmen.

Bolan took a quick accounting of what was going on.

Tonne had five men with him when he tore off into the building, disengaging from the crossfire between the Executioner and the concussion-shocked remnants of Kilo's contingent.

Kilo was coming on with four men of his own, worst case scenario.

From what Bolan could confirm, there were still seventeen gunmen on the loose. Kilo might not have been in the best condition, as might some of the others, but seventeen guns were still a hard force to deal with. The Executioner noted two more bodies, which lowered the enemy's forces to fifteen. Nappico had obviously picked up some replacement firepower for the weapons he'd left behind on the dock.

"Tony," Bolan whispered. "On your level now. What's the interrogation room number you're in?"

"Five," Nappico returned softly. "Got movement."

Bolan had left Nappico's AR in the river. There was little sense running around with three weapons, and the second rifle was simply just a prop, a means of impressing Kilo and Tonne while confronting them and setting up a battle that he could win. He'd also kicked Nappico's spare ammo off the dock simply to avoid confusion. Jamming in a magazine of 5.56 mm into a rifle chambered for .300 caliber would be tantamount to suicide.

He shouldered the rifle, still low, barely exposing himself. He could see that there were three gunmen, moving slowly, carefully, seeking out Nappico and his daughter. They'd open a door and then they'd fire, dragging out the corpse of a Haitian prisoner, as a flag that the room had been cleared.

The prison breakout was executed, as Bolan had surmised with all the evidence gained to date, to seek out and punish those who either had betrayed Le Loupe Grotte, or had simply failed in their mission to command the streets of West Palm Beach in the face of their enemies.

The dead, and soon-to-be-dead, were slowing the search for Nappico and his daughter. That gave the Executioner all the edge he needed. He lined up the sights, pressed the trigger and speared a bullet through the ear of one of the gunmen, a Cartel thug whose head flopped over and seemed to deflate as his brains exited through the other side of his skull.

Suddenly, the search for the cop and their former hostage was called off, and the survivors around Bolan's sniper victim were spraying lead toward the stairwell and rushing for what cover they could find. Too bad for them that Bolan was only inches off the floor, using it and the top step as cover as he lined up a second shot and put a full-auto burst through the chest of a shotgunner who tromboned the slide of his weapon while screaming.

The Haitian shotgunner was thrown back, his heart and spine destroyed by the precision burst. With that man's fall, the Executioner's free ambush was going to take a lot more effort as gunfire lowered toward him, aiming at the floor, but from their angle, they were ricocheting bullets over his head, coming too close for comfort. Bolan triggered another burst and smashed out the knee of an enemy shooter, collapsing him to the ground. One fire burst and the fallen gangster was finished off.

Of course, since the enemy was presently concentrating on Bolan, Nappico kicked open a door and opened fire on the distracted gunmen. He leaned into the burst, sweeping a trio of men across the smalls of their backs. He emptied his magazine and sawed the three of them in two, severing their spines, dropping them to the ground.

Bolan reloaded and scanned the area. "Skruggs still alive?"

Nappico looked back. "Yeah. Looks like he's the only one, though."

Bolan frowned. "No, there are two more members of the Chief Dozen still alive. And they haven't come up here yet."

Nappico narrowed his eyes. "So you wouldn't mind if Skruggs were a sole survivor."

"I'd insist on it," the Executioner returned. He pulled out his CPDA and sent the signal to Brognola to send in SWAT and ambulances to secure the building. "Jessie, stay here and lock the door. Police will be by in a few minutes."

The frightened girl nodded, wide-eyed at the murderers sprawled in bloody heaps around the floor.

Bolan turned to Nappico. "Let's get moving."

16

Bolan led the way back downstairs, reloading as he did so. Nappico could tell that they were heading toward the station's motor pool, meaning that Kilo and Tonne might be making a getaway. It was the only logical conclusion, as the battle at the dock showed that they didn't have any boats ready for action.

That meant that they would be driving out, and since the parking lot was visible to the street, that left only the garage where the police stored their working vehicles out of the elements and away from prying eyes and break-ins. During their movement, Bolan reloaded the Blackout, and handed Nappico the 12-gauge Remington since the cop had only had two magazines for the folded-stock AK he'd torn into the gunmen with.

"They're not going to get away," Nappico said, thumbing shells out of spare USAS-12 magazines and putting them in his 870. "If it comes to me or them, let me die. Just murder the fuck out of those two bastards."

"I don't sacrifice my allies," Bolan returned. "And I'm not going to give them the opportunity to start a chase."

"Please remember that," Nappico told him. He had the shotgun topped off by the time they heard the sudden flurry of gunfire rattling inside the parking garage.

"What the hell?" Nappico asked.

Bolan peeked around the corner using a small hand mirror. "It's Kilo and his gang. They're shooting it out with someone inside the garage."

"Who?" Nappico asked.

"Tonne. He left Kilo behind when we caught them between my rifle and your grenades," Bolan surmised. He smirked. "Kilo's down to one man, but he's not giving up."

"Give me a shot," Nappico said.

Bolan mused over it for a second, then waved him into position. "Just Kilo...or..."

With the first syllable, Nappico was up, Remington thundering, catching Kilo and his surviving partner from behind. The cop's first charge of No. 4 buck was low and to the right, crashing into Kilo's last surviving gunman at hip level, destroying his pelvis. Kilo jerked violently at the roar of the shotgun, clutching his thigh as it caught some .24-caliber pellets.

Kilo was torn between continuing to defend himself from Tonne and his gunners and addressing the new threat that popped up from behind. Nappico didn't give the Haitian thug a chance to make that decision, racking the slide and aiming higher, this time putting his swarm of copper-jacketed lead right into Kilo's sternum. Body armor buckled under the impact of more than twenty projectiles and nearly a ton of kinetic energy, making the Haitian mobster crash awkwardly through the door he'd been shooting only a moment before.

Off balance, bloody and already weakened by a combination of concussion grenade assault and a steel butt stock across the jaw, Kilo was caught in the back by a swarm of Tonne's bullets. Some were stopped by Kilo's vest, but then the mobster's head snapped forward, ejecting a halo of crimson droplets as his shoelace-braided locks flew under the impact of something big and powerful striking the back of his skull.

It looked as if Kilo had been crucified, pinned on a cross of lead and fire.

Nappico pumped the Remington again and fired just to make certain. This burst of buckshot erased Kilo's head from his shoulders. Decapitated, the mobster dropped to the concrete like a marionette with its strings cut. The mutilated mess on the floor signalled a pause in the shooting.

Nappico's heart hammered in his rib cage, and his breathing was deep and ragged.

Bolan pulled the cop out of the way, sitting him down.

"What?" Nappico asked.

"You caught a bullet," Bolan said, tearing open the wounded man's shirt. Luckily, the bullet had struck him in the side of his belly, punching into muscle and fat rather than penetrating into his intestines.

Nappico looked down.

"While Tonne was finishing off Kilo, you took a bullet, maybe one that went through him," Bolan said. "Probably what deflected it enough to give you a nonvital wound."

Nappico grimaced. "Go get Tonne!"

Bolan pushed the tattered rags of Nappico's shirt into his hand. "Apply pressure so you don't bleed out."

"Go!" Nappico shouted.

To the cop's credit, he was leaning on the wad of cloth and making it a solid pressure dressing.

With that, Matt Cooper rose and spun toward the parking garage, pulling a hand grenade from his kit.

WITH NAPPICO ATTENDING TO his own injuries, and ambulances on their way, Bolan was alone and free to cut loose with everything at his disposal. He primed the M-67 hand grenade and hurled it down the hall and out into the garage.

The Executioner didn't have to worry about shrapnel harming Nappico, let alone his daughter, because Bolan had hurled the minibomb with all of his might, sailing it past the corpse of Kilo to where it would land amid the pillars of the parking lot. With a mighty crash, the grenade went off.

It was only one man who was caught at ground zero for the detonation, and his corpse was swept off its feet, hurled sidelong into another pillar where his mangled body was wrapped brutally around the concrete post. The grenade had been intended to put heads down and stop the enemy's shooting, and it worked just as the warrior had planned. Bolan was in the entrance to the parking garage, rifle tracking, when he spotted a battered Haitian, clutching the side of his face where shrapnel hadn't been moving fast enough to kill, but was sufficient to wound.

This guy, however, didn't know when to quit. He had an Uzi machine pistol clamped in one hand and was firing it sideways. It was a notorious shooting method of gangsters, and Bolan wasn't surprised that the initial burst from the man's chatter box was off target by feet, peppering the concrete cinder-block wall ineffectually.

The Executioner showed the Haitian what marksmanship on full-auto was all about, swiveling and taking him with two short bursts, one crushing his pelvis, the other chewing off his head as his crippled form began to collapse into the line of fire.

That was two of Tonne's group down, but Bolan hadn't known how many had survived the battle with Kilo. In the garage, there were plenty of places for a gunman to take cover, and the Executioner slid to a halt behind a pillar.

At that moment a spray of auto fire ripped the air, pounding at the concrete shaft Bolan had ducked behind. It was a short flurry of gunfire, meaning that this guy had more discipline on the trigger than the other gunner that he'd taken down.

Bolan let the Blackout drop to the ground, tossing it so that it was out in the open on the far right of the column he used as his shield. Even as the weapon flew, Bolan plucked the Beretta 93-R from its shoulder holster, thumbed the selector to burst-mode, and whipped around the corner in the opposite direction the moment his rifle clattered on the ground.

The shooter spun toward the sound of the rifle hitting the floor, distracted by the noise and movement. This bought the Executioner a few moments and three long strides to get a better angle on his opponent. The Haitian gunman jerked back, alert to Bolan's ruse, but it was too late for him as 9 mm rounds snarled through the blunt suppressor attached to the Beretta's barrel, three shots walking up the man's breastbone. High-velocity 9 mm hollowpoints crunched through bone and cartilege to rupture lung tissue and sever the gunman's aorta.

It was a brutal, swift end for the shooter, dropping him to the floor as dead meat.

The soldier kicked the corpse's gun away from lifeless hands. It was an instinctive motion he did when he passed by any fallen enemy. Just to make certain, he flicked his weapon back to semi-auto and punched a single round between the lifeless form's closed eyes, destroying his brain.

Bolan had seen more than a few foes fake dead.

"Hey, is it too late to take you up on that offer from before?" a voice called out from some hidden spot.

It was Tonne. He sounded out of breath, his voice was raised in pitch and sounded nervous.

"What? A quick death?" Bolan called back.

"A chance to walk away," Tonne said.

Bolan sighed. "You know you're just stalling. You've got some way out of here. And if you can, you'll shoot me as soon as you make the break."

The Executioner cursed the acoustics in the garage, echoes rebounding making it difficult to pinpoint where Tonne's voice was coming from. He crouched and grabbed the shirt of the man he'd just put down and hefted him up. There would be one sure way to get Tonne to reveal his position.

With a hard yank, be brought up the Haitian corpse and poked him out from behind the concrete pillar. In an instant, a powerful, booming weapon split the air, the same powerhouse impact that had busted open the back of Kilo's head before Nappico took it completely off with the shotgun.

The dead Haitian bounced against Bolan's shoulder. He let the corpse fall away, looking toward an SUV where a second muzzle-flash emerged. This time the bullet struck concrete, pulverizing it and spraying the Executioner with dust and stone splinters. Bolan ducked around and scrambled to a second pillar even as third and fourth shots smashed fist-size holes in the column.

Then there was a tinkle of brass bouncing on concrete. Bolan realized that Tonne was packing some kind of Magnum revolver, and if he was down to that, he was running out of options. The SUV door opened.

Bolan rose, pumping two bursts into the rear window of the distant SUV, shattering safety glass with six full-auto rounds. That brought another Magnum slug screaming close, smashing the wall with enough violence to create a crater the size of a dinner plate.

The Executioner didn't flinch. He'd been on the giving and receiving end of Magnum gunfire more times than he could dare to count. He simply made use of the Beretta's fold-down grip and extra-length barrel to provide him with superior accuracy. Skidding behind a third column, he saw that Tonne was working his way back into the driver's seat.

Even as Bolan spied him, Tonne fired another shot. His right arm, however, was dangling useless at his side, tied off with a rag. He must have taken a shot earlier, probably nailed when the Executioner had leaped backward into the river.

The Haitian couldn't shoot and drive at the same time, so Bolan put the Beretta away and stayed low. Tonne grimaced, then leaned into the driver's seat, turning the key in the ignition. This brief moment gave Bolan all the room he needed to rise and dash toward the vehicle.

Tonne sat up after working the gear shift, then glanced over his shoulder. The Executioner was there, jumping up onto the running board before the Haitian could reach for his revolver on the dashboard. Bolan had drawn two of his blades, one a crowbar-style utility blade, the other his fighting knife. The crowbar was reversed because it had a glass breaker and Bolan punched out hard, shattering the driver's-side window.

Cubes of safety glass sprayed into Tonne's face under the impact of the hardened pommel, but the Haitian gangster still had enough wits to stomp on the gas and accelerate out of the parking spot. The only trouble with Tonne's plan was that Bolan speared the chisel-like blade of the crowbar into the driver's seat, anchoring himself in place even as the SUV charged toward the exit.

Tonne was torn between steering and reaching for his handgun, but he kept his head and didn't move his hand from the wheel, realizing that he could use the vehicle to get rid of the Executioner. Tires squealed and he turned toward a pillar.

Bolan knew he only had a few moments before he would be scraped off against a concrete post at forty miles an hour. That was why he had a knife in each hand. With a surge of strength, hanging on to the driver's seat, Bolan leaned in and thrust his combat blade toward Tonne. The point speared into the Haitian's rib cage, snagging on bone for a moment, but Bolan's strength was enough to overcome that resistance.

Blood splashed over Tonne's lips, and he jerked reflexively. The SUV overshot its mark, veering into a pillar on the passenger-side fender. That impact jarred Bolan off both blade handles, hurling him to the ground. Only the warrior's lithe muscles and catlike reflexes kept him from landing wrong. He rolled, twisting to deflect collision from the ground and spare his bones dozens of fractures.

The SUV, on the other hand, rebounded into another concrete post. This time, though, instead of a glancing blow, it struck, grille first, and stopped, but only after turning concrete into dust and bending rebar like it were taffy.

Bolan did a quick evaluation of himself as he struggled back to his feet. Sure, he'd managed to land so that he didn't snap bones, but his back and thighs were hammered, and would soon become huge masses of bruises.

But he could walk, albeit painfully. His limbs responded to his mental commands.

Bolan staggered over to the crashed SUV. Rebar strands had carved through the nose of the vehicle and were bent around the engine. The windshield was completely opaque, broken and cracked safety glass turned white from the multitude of fractures that ran through it. He looked at the driver's seat, and Tonne was slumped, glaring hatefully out the window.

The Executioner couldn't see the handle of his knife, but there was an ugly, wide gash in the man's chest where the blade had penetrated. Peering down, he could see the bloodied, bent weapon lying in Tonne's lap. The Haitian continued breathing by sure willpower and rage alone, not that it gave him the strength to reach for anything. The Magnum revolver he'd dumped onto the dash was gone, lost in the crash.

"Who are you, man?" Tonne asked.

Bolan pulled the Desert Eagle from its holster. "I'm a debt collector."

"And what…I owe you?" Tonne continued. His ire only deepened at Bolan's cryptic, annoying response.

"For the deaths of too many people," Bolan said. He raised the .44 Magnum and dropped the hammer.

Tonne's face imploded as the hollowpoint smashed into it.

Sirens sounded in the distance. They were on their way a lot sooner than Bolan had anticipated, but he figured that with all of the grenades and gunfire, someone might have called in an alert.

This was his cue to disappear.

There would be a plane waiting for him at the airport, and with a little luck, the Executioner would have a week or so to recuperate from his cuts and bruises before he was needed again.

But he doubted it.

War Everlasting would always be nagging at Mack Bolan's conscience.

* * * * *